TO

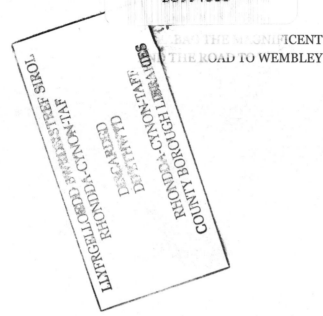

... BA'S THE MAGNIFICENT
... THE ROAD TO WEMBLEY

By the same author:
Under the Cindertip

Teabag the Magnificent and the Road to Wembley

Nigel Morgan

First published in 2014

© Nigel Morgan

© Gwasg Carreg Gwalch 2014

Published with the financial support
of the Welsh Books Council

ISBN: 978-1-84527-467-2

Cover design: Welsh Books Council

Gwasg Carreg Gwalch, 12 Iard yr Orsaf,
Llanrwst, Wales, LL26 0EH
Tel: 01492 642031
e-mail:books@carreg-gwalch.com
Website: www.carreg-gwalch.com

To Lisa, for her constant support,
and to all our children.

Huge thanks to Carreg Gwalch,
and in particular to Jen Llywelyn.

Brandy, our scuffy little apricot poodle,
was the inspiration. She is Teabag.
Diolch yn fawr iawn – and blessings.

Chapter One

Shivering in his seat, on the sidelines, on a bleak day in January, Jimmy reminded himself that he was about to watch a football match, nothing more! He knew that it wasn't a matter of life or death, yet his tummy churned in a sickly, too-much-ice-cream-and-chocolate sort of way.

Like everyone else in the village of Barrowmarsh, Jimmy and his twin sister Jenny had wished, hoped and prayed for this moment; they'd allowed themselves to dream, but they'd never imagined it could happen.

Now they watched from their seats as the referee checked his watch and signalled to his assistants that everything was ready for the match to start.

The village players, in white shirts and black shorts, gathered in a team huddle for the captain's pep-talk. Then, with shouts of encouragement, the players ran to their positions to face up to eleven very impressive and famous footballers.

Jimmy glanced at his sister. She was studying the anxious faces of other spectators. They knew that every one of the other team's players, kitted out in those incredibly well-known and world-famous red shirts, was an international star.

Their very own village team, Barrowmarsh Thursdays, was about to take on the most powerful and the most successful team in the whole wide world!

'Oh boy, we're going to get slaughtered,' Jimmy muttered.

Jenny shuddered. 'I'm absolutely terrified. I can't bear to look!'

Jimmy swallowed hard. 'Who would have thought, back in November, that we would have reached this stage of the FA Cup?' He bit down on his lip and shook his head as he remembered where this adventure had started ...

It had been the previous November, the day after Hallowe'en ... It was a dismally overcast Saturday afternoon and it had been pouring since the night before. It was a murky, miserable day; a wringing wet and wildly windy day; a puddle and splash, soaking-socks-and-scarf sort of day.

Jimmy looked down in dismay at the sausage from his hot dog. The rain was washing the tomato sauce off, and the bread roll was soaked and soggy. And he knew that when he got back to the side of the pitch, where Jenny was waiting for him, she'd make her Miss Smartypants face and tell him that he should have bought some chocolate instead.

He splashed through muddy puddles to the recycling area. 'Yuck, how can ducks eat bread that's been thrown into the water?' he said, finishing off the sausage and dropping the soft, squidgy roll into the bin.

He trudged back towards the pitch to watch the last part of the match; the wave of grumbling from the crowd didn't sound hopeful.

Jimmy didn't have far to go when the heavens opened yet again. Some of the crowd attempted to shelter under dripping umbrellas. Others stood huddled together in soggy coats and scarves, with their hands in their pockets, and battered by the torrential downpour. There was no grandstand at Barrowmarsh; no shelter, no warm clubhouse, just a low, wooden fence around a muddy pitch. There wasn't even a proper dressing room; the players changed in a back room of a local guest house.

'Welcome to Druid's Park,' Jimmy thought, wiping rain from his eyes. 'It's not exactly Barcelona ... but it's our home ground; the home of Barrowmarsh Thursdays Football Club, members of the Welsh Central and Borders League, Division Three!'

'Another dismal performance from The Thursdays,' complained a voice in the crowd.

'Come on, midfield, get a grip!' shouted someone else. 'What's the matter, got two left feet?'

Early in the game Barrowmarsh had scored an easy goal to take the lead. A second goal led the supporters to predict a walkover. But as time trickled by, the team's performance seemed to go from bad to worse, and Barrowmarsh had to defend desperately as their opponents threw everything into attack.

Jimmy looked at his watch. The game was now moving into the last ten minutes and the home team's exhausted players were still clinging to their fragile two-goal advantage.

'Watch out, they're looking dangerous!' someone shouted. Seconds later there was a collective groan as a lanky, lolloping forward bundled the ball into the bottom of the Barrowmarsh net.

Jimmy peered between spectators. Geraint, the

Barrowmarsh goalkeeper, lay in the gooey mud. He looked totally fed up. Jimmy got back to his place to find Jenny and Grandad sheltering under a huge golf umbrella.

'Where've you been?' Jenny asked. 'I'm freezing and I think I'm going to die of ...' she pulled out a small hard-covered journal, which she called her Treasure Book, and flipped a few pages, '... of hypothermia! And, I've finished my chocolate; got any sweets?'

'Nope, sorry, sis.'

Jenny and Jimmy Jones were twins, almost identical, eleven years and one month old and born within minutes of each other. Everyone told them they were like two peas in a pod, but they were quick to deny it. 'OK, our hair may be the same colour, but she wears hers in a pony-tail,' Jimmy would protest.

'And he's a boy!' Jenny would add.

The only thing they agreed on was the colour of their eyes – green – and the shape of their noses. Mum said they were lucky to have her nose and not Dad's! 'This is a centre-back's nose,' Dad would growl, 'smashed into shape by a hundred strikers' heads', and he'd carry on reading his newspaper in a 'humph' sort of way.

Mum and Dad owned and ran Druid's Lodge Guest House, which Grandad and Grandma used to keep before they retired and moved next door. Dad was also the manager of Barrowmarsh Thursdays, and a key defender. Important, maybe, but the most important member of the Jones family was their rag-tag, scruffy little dog called Teabag.

'Come on, ref, blow your whistle,' urged Grandad.

'We can't hold on for much longer ... Oh, no, another corner ... Well saved, Geraint – he's the only one awake. The rest of them are as useful as chocolate teapots!' He winked at the twins.

Jimmy winked back, and Jenny grinned. She looked around, rubbed her hands together briskly, and shivered. 'I'm bored. Let's go up to Sam's to see his snake.'

'Hang on – it's not over yet,' said Jimmy, craning his neck and looking past his sister. 'Go on, Mr Frost, get stuck in.'

Jenny folded her arms and sighed as her brother squeezed past to lean against the fence.

Mr Frost, the twins' class teacher, played in midfield for Barrowmarsh Thursdays, but he wasn't doing too much playing at that moment; he was sitting on the ground, covered in mud, having been on the receiving end of a heavy tackle. Jimmy looked back over his shoulder. 'I think he's hurt his knee. He's making a horrible face.'

Jenny joined him at the fence. 'Yes, the physiotherapist is splashing water on it.' She tried to copy Mr Frost's 'ouch' expression.

After a minute or two, the injured teacher was helped off the field. 'It must be serious if he's coming off,' said Grandad.

Jimmy stepped back under the golf umbrella. 'Grandad, what's a fizzy ... fizzy ... fizzy old terrorist?'

Jenny darted under the umbrella and flicked through her Treasure Book. 'Look, this is the word. I think you mean physiotherapist.'

Grandad laughed and winked at them.

'Well, anyway,' Jimmy said, 'I expect he's glad to get out of the mud and rain.'

'Bad luck, Freddy,' Grandad called.

'Yes, well done, Mr Frost.' The twins watched as their teacher left the field and limped towards Druid's Lodge for treatment and a shower.

'Well done?' jeered a man standing slightly apart from the crowd behind the Barrowmarsh goal. He was clapping ... very slowly. His eyes were narrowed, and his mouth was tight, as if he'd tasted something horrible.

'When we say 'well done' that's what we mean,' muttered Jimmy, looking across to the slow-clapping man, 'but Mr Braine says one thing and means something completely different.'

Jenny nodded. 'If we did it we'd get into trouble for telling fibs, but Mr Braine does it all the time.'

Jimmy scratched his soaked head. 'Dad calls him the Sarcastic Clapper'.'

Jenny tucked her journal inside her coat. 'You're right, bro, but Mum says Mr Braine isn't telling fibs, he's just being sarcastic, and I've written it in my Treasure Book.'

Mr Braine never missed a match, but whenever Barrowmarsh were losing or playing badly, which was quite often, he would clap his hands very slowly and say things like, 'Excellent, Barrowmarsh; that's it, that's the way. Go on; give the ball to the other team. Why don't you just score in your own goal and have done with it?'

Now he mockingly applauded a shot from the opposition's striker which rattled the cross-bar, before a Barrowmarsh player booted the ball to safety.

'Blow the whistle, ref,' someone yelled. 'Put us out of our misery!'

Mr Braine shook his head and began a one-man slow handclap. 'Brilliant!' he mocked. 'Just send them a written invitation to score, why don't you.'

Jimmy looked over at Mr Brain and frowned. 'There he goes again. What's the matter with him?'

Grandad puffed out his cheeks and shook his head. 'Wayne Braine might be one of my oldest friends, but look at him ... a face like a camel sucking a lemon.'

The twins sniggered.

Meanwhile, Matthew Henderson, the Barrowmarsh substitute, stood at the edge of the pitch, waiting to take the place of the injured Mr Frost.

'Go for it, Matty,' Grandad shouted from under the umbrella, 'show 'em what you can do.'

'I don't think he wants to go on, Grandad,' said Jimmy. 'He's got his hands up inside his sleeves, his teeth are going clackety-clack, and water is dripping off his nose.'

He moved to the sideline, closer to the Barrowmarsh sub. 'What are you looking at, squirt?' Matthew growled.

Jimmy shrugged and turned to Jenny. 'Why is he always so horrible?'

'Mum says it's because he wears a baseball cap back-to-front,' Jenny replied. 'She says he's got teenage attitude.'

'Well then, I'm *glad* he has to go onto the pitch in all this freezing-cold rain!'

Mr Braine started his slow hand-clapping again. 'That's right; well done, Coach, very well done indeed.

We need to help our overworked defence and you send on an attacking mid-fielder; excellent tactics, well done!'

Jimmy chuckled. 'I think he's being sarcastic again,'

Jenny giggled, their grandad winked, the referee blew his whistle ... and Barrowmarsh won by a whisker, sending them into the first round of the FA Cup!

Chapter Two

Monday Morning and there had been no guests staying at Druid's Lodge the night before, so Dad, who usually cooked breakfast for visitors, was sitting in the kitchen, engrossed in the sports page of the morning newspaper.

Mum worked in the school office every week-day morning. She whizzed through the kitchen, grabbing her bag from the table. 'Your clean T-shirts and shorts are on the hall table; don't forget them ... are you listening, Jimmy?'

'Eh, what?'

'Your PE things! Put them in your bag, oh, and here's your dinner money for the week.' She dropped some notes and coins onto the kitchen table.

Jenny picked up the money. 'Okay, Mum.'

'We go through this routine every Monday Morning,' Jenny mumbled under her breath, passing a piece of toast to a tail-wagging Teabag. 'Mum gives us dinner money to take to school; we take it in, then we give it in at the school office ... to Mum!'

'I think it's stupid,' Jimmy whispered, lobbing another piece of toast Teabag's way. 'When we get to school we just give it back to her! Crazy or what?'

'She wants us to be treated like everyone else at school,' said Jenny. 'If she took our money in for us it might seem like favouritism.'

'I suppose so,' Jimmy agreed.

Jenny finished jotting a few notes in her Treasure

Book. 'I asked Mr Frost about it, and he told me that it teaches us to take responsibility, and shows that Mum trusts us to do a job properly.'

Jimmy nodded.

Jenny flicked a few pages of her journal. 'Teachers are trained to say positive and encouraging things.'

Mum whooshed back through the kitchen. 'Come on, Jimmy, hurry up, Jenny, get a move on ... has anyone seen my car keys?'

The twins shrugged and said that they hadn't.

'Jack?' Mum snapped.

Dad sniffed, blinked, and looked up from his newspaper. 'Eh, what's that?'

'My car keys, have you seen them?'

'Um ... uh.' He scratched his nose and looked from Jimmy to Jenny to Mum.

'For goodness sake, Jack, do you think you could tear yourself away from the sports page for just one second?' She rubbed the back of her neck and sighed.

'What? What are you on about?' Dad had obviously not heard a single thing Mum had said. He stretched and pointed to the newspaper. 'There's a small report here on the FA Cup qualifying matches and ...'

'I don't know what I'm going to do with you, Jack Jones.'

Mum's eyes narrowed but the twins could see she was smiling just a little bit.

'Your head, Jack, is full of football!'

Jimmy looked at Jenny and they grinned. 'Imagine Dad with a football on his shoulders where his head should be.'

Jenny's eyes twinkled. 'Yes, a football with eyes and a nose, and with a mouth and ears.'

They laughed and Teabag yapped and wagged his tail.

'*Jack*!' Mum shouted, 'Have you seen my car keys? I'm going to be late for work.'

'But the school is just a two-minute walk away!' Dad scratched his chin. 'You can see it from our window; why are you taking the car?'

Mum sighed, then tutted. 'Well, I know the school's only a short walk away. I'm not taking the car, but my lipstick, the one that I absolutely need today, is in the glove compartment.'

'Mum?' Jenny pulled out her journal and a pencil. 'Why do you call it a glove compartment when you only ever keep lipstick and sweets in it?'

'NOT NOW, JENNIFER ... I'M LATE!'

Jimmy had a sudden thought. 'I think I know where your keys might be.' He slid across the kitchen to Teabag's basket, pulled out a blue, fluffy blanket and there they were – Mum's car keys.

'*That dog*!' Mum shrieked.

Teabag wagged his tail and the twins grinned again.

Mum grabbed her keys and shot to the back door, calling back over her shoulder as she went, 'Make sure that pest of a dog is inside when you leave for school; we don't want him following us again. The last time was so embarrassing!'

Teabag wagged his tail and his mouth hung open in a smiley sort of way.

'Grandad will pop in to take him for a walk ... bye, see you later,' and she zoomed off to answer the phone, open letters, take dinner money and do all sorts of other important things school secretaries do.

Jenny's eyes widened and she put her hand to her cheek. 'Do you remember the last time Teabag followed us to school?'

'Not half!' Jimmy giggled. 'He sneaked into school when Geraint, the postman, opened the door.'

They laughed together, remembering how Mum had spotted Teabag running down the corridor, and had raced after him, calling him a little pest, only to see him galloping into assembly, tail wagging.

Jenny's grin widened. 'Do you remember what happened next? It has to be the funniest thing that has ever happened in assembly!'

Jimmy was laughing so much that he could only gesture that Teabag had run over to the piano, wagged his tail, and lifted his back leg ...

'All Things Bright and Beautiful', shrieked Jenny, 'Mrs Morping was playing 'All Things Bright and Beautiful' ...' The twins were laughing hysterically at the memory, and Jimmy drummed his feet on the floor.

'And the puddle from the poodle spread ...' gasped Jimmy.

'And Miss Bell sang, 'All things bright and beautiful, all creatures great and small – TAKE THAT WRETCHED ANIMAL; REMOVE HIM FROM THIS HALL!'

The twins fell against the table, wheezing, shaking, and laughing uncontrollably. Teabag, the scruffy little apricot poodle, with a face like a teddy bear, bounced around them enjoying the fun, and barking happily.

Dad, however, poked his nose over his newspaper, frowned, blinked rapidly, and said, 'You can laugh now, but your mother gave us some serious grief over that, so make sure the smelly mutt doesn't follow you again. Come on, look sharp and get off to school.'

Jimmy and Jenny arrived at the school playground and saw their friend, Sam.

'Hi, Sam,' they said together.

'I've got three new badges, look.' Sam frowned, pulled a small package from his school bag and brought out the shiny badges.

It was quite normal for Sam to say only what he wanted to say. The twins didn't mind at all because that was what he did. Megan, Sam's teaching assistant, told them that he liked to do things in his own way, and that he was 'an individual.' The twins knew that Sam had a medical condition that sometimes made him think and do things in a different way to most people. Everyone knew that he was absolutely brilliant at Maths and could work out things much quicker than Mr Frost.

Jenny and Jimmy looked at Sam's badges. He collected all sorts; it was his favourite hobby. Sam often got upset when someone he didn't know came to talk to him, but the twins were his friends.

He was lucky to have such a lovely and sparkly teaching assistant as Megan. She really understood Sam's different ways. Once, when she came to school with curly hair instead of her usual straight style, Sam refused to speak to her or even look at her. And, if he got very upset and sat under the table, Megan would sit with him until he was ready to come out.

The playground was getting busier as the usual Monday morning rush got underway. Parents, some with babies in buggies, handed lunch boxes and book-bags to their children. Older pupils gathered in groups and greeted their friends; some kicked footballs around and others swung PE bags as they chased and played.

Sam was still showing everyone his new badges when Megan came through the gate with Mrs Morping.

Megan waved. 'Hi gang.' She was wearing a bright yellow pullover and her long, dark hair was tied into a ponytail with a yellow scarf. Sam liked yellow and green. He didn't mind red but really hated blue, so Megan never wore blue.

'Morning, Sam,' said Megan.

'I've got three new badges.' Sam held out his hand to show her.

'Wow,' Megan smiled, 'that'll make you a happy chappy.'

The twins laughed; they liked the things Megan said, like when she called everyone her 'munchkins'.

Mrs Morping pulled her wheelie-trolley behind her and chatted with Megan as they walked up the ramp towards the school's entrance.

Mr Frost hobbled out of the main door with the bell in his hand. 'Bore da, Mildred, bore da, Megan.' He smiled and held the door open for the two ladies.

'Looks like Mr Frost is crocked from that knock he picked up on Saturday,' Jimmy said to Jenny.

Jenny frowned. 'You're right, bro, hope he's okay.'

'Bore da, plant; here we go, here we go, here we go,' Mr Frost sang. 'Are we all ready for another exciting week in the land of learning?' He chuckled and looked around the playground.

Jimmy noticed that their teacher always seemed to have a smile on his face – well, except for when he was having a quiet word with Nails. Norman Nailsworthy was in the same class as the twins and Sam. He liked to be known as 'Nails' and said the name suited him because he was the toughest boy in the school and as hard as nails! He'd only been in Barrowmarsh since earlier that year, so was fairly new. Sometimes he laughed at Sam and tried to make fun, but none of the other youngsters took any notice.

'Bore da, Mr Frost, did you hurt your leg badly in the match last Saturday?' Jenny asked.

'Please, sir,' Nails mimicked in a high and squeaky voice, 'did you hurt your leg playing pathetic football?'

The teacher glanced across at Nails and then turned his head towards Jenny. 'It's not too bad, Jennifer, diolch yn fawr iawn. It's my knee, actually, but I'm hoping it'll be fine for the next match; another very big game on Saturday, of course, the FA Cup first round. I can't wait.' He grinned broadly.

'I've got three new badges.' Sam held them out to Mr Frost.

'Fantastic, Sam, you'll have to show everyone during Circle Time later on, and tell us all about them.'

Nails, hands tucked in his pockets and shoulders hunched, slouched past.

Mr Frost looked up and smiled warmly. 'Bore da, Norman.'

Nails just sniffed. 'Hurt yourself playing football for the cripples, Mr Frost, *Sir*?' He always seemed to have a sneering and somehow disrespectful way of saying *Sir*.

'I'm doing fine, thank you, Norman, as are the team ... it's the FA Cup first round on Saturday. It is something that the whole village of Barrowmarsh can be extremely proud of.'

'FA Cup?' Nails rolled his eyes and smirked. 'You're having a laugh; you'll be slaughtered, as usual.'

Mr Frost smiled. 'We'll see, Norman, we'll see.'

Nails snarled. 'Stinking football!'

Just then a loud *VROOOOOM* made everyone turn their heads towards the playground entrance. An enormous silver and black motorbike glided gracefully through the school's opened gates. John, the lollipop man, stood with his arms outstretched, gesturing for the pupils and parents to keep back, allowing the bike to enter the school grounds and turn slowly into a parking space.

The bike's engine was switched off and the gleaming machine shuddered then purred to silence. The rider nimbly dismounted, pulling off enormous, black leather gloves. Displayed on the back of the matching leather jacket was a sinister looking skull, surrounded by red and yellow flames, together with the words 'Nell's Angels', written in silver studs. On the back of the shiny crash helmet was a white skull and crossbones emblem!

The biker turned towards the watching crowd, and in pulling off the protective helmet revealed a mop of unruly grey hair, like frizzy wire wool, thick, black-framed glasses and the smiling face of a very small and very elderly lady.

'*BORE DA, MY LITTLE BLOSSOMS*,' she boomed in a deep thunderous voice that you really wouldn't have expected to belong to such a small and elderly lady.

'Bore da, Miss Bell,' everyone called back, delightedly.

The booming-voiced biker was none other than the head teacher – or headmistress as she insisted on being called – of Ysgol Gynradd Cors y Domen – Barrowmarsh Primary School, Miss Nelly Bell.

An adoring crowd gathered around Miss Bell and there was no shortage of volunteers to help carry her belongings into school.

Mr Frost chuckled as he walked over to the headmistress. 'Bore da, Nell, can I help you with anything?'

'Bore da, Frederick, it's all sorted, diolch; the little darlings seem to have everything in hand ... Tahir,' Miss Bell called after one of the helpers, 'make sure you put my ignition keys on my desk where I'll be able to find them ... shan't be able to start the Hog without them.'

'They'll be safely on your desk, Miss Bell,' the boy replied, smiling.

'Diolch yn fawr iawn, Tahir.'

The headmistress turned to her beloved Harley-Davidson motor-bike, patted it fondly and kissed the handle-bars. 'Now stay here and be a good Hog for Mummy.'

Jenny nudged her brother and pointed to Mr Frost, who was limping quite badly as he hobbled across the playground. 'It doesn't look good; do you think he'll be fit enough to play in Saturday's match?'

Jimmy folded his arms and shook his head, slowly. 'I'm not sure, but Dad will be gutted if Mr Frost is unable to play.'

Jenny nodded. 'He's our team captain and our best mid-fielder. Barrowmarsh can't afford to be without him.'

'Come on,' said Jimmy, 'grab your bag, the bell is about to go.'

Chapter Three

'Don't forget the dinner money, sis,' Jimmy reminded Jenny.

She dug into her bag and pulled out her Cath Kidston purse. 'I won't, don't worry.'

Sam was showing his badges to Yunara, another friend, when Mr Frost rang the bell. 'Time to go in, everybody, another exciting day beckons.'

'Whatever,' Nails scowled. He didn't move other than to pull his hands from his pockets and to kick a small stone across the playground.

'Quickly, Norman,' Mr Frost called.

'Humph!' was the only response from Nails.

'Come along, Norman. We're all going inside; you won't want to be left out here on your own.'

'Humph!'

'Let's not be misanthropic, Norman,' Mr Frost said, pleasantly.

'Awesome!' gasped Jenny. There was a frantic flurry as she plunged her hands into her school-bag. 'Where are my dictionary and my Treasure Book? Mis ... misan ... misanthrop ... here it is ... *Misanthropic ... Avoiding or hating human company* ... I am *so* going to use this word!'

Jenny saw that Mr Frost wasn't going to give up. 'You are going to have a great day, Norman, believe me.'

'I won't,' Nails kicked another stone across the school yard.

'Well, let's just wait and see, shall we?' Mr Frost smiled. 'Positive thinking, Norman, positive thinking.'

Nails walked slowly up the ramp to the school's entrance and Mr Frost followed him, whistling the tune of *Match of the Day*.

'I'm just going to give this dinner money to Mum, er, I mean to the school clerk,' Jenny corrected.

'Okay, sis, see you in class.' Jimmy strolled off down the corridor with Sam and Yunara.

Straight after morning registration everyone filed into the hall for assembly. Jenny noticed that Miss Bell, who stood at the front, was wearing a tweed suit, a lilac shawl and a pair of dainty brown shoes in place of the huge black and buckled boots she'd had on when she'd arrived on her Hog earlier that morning.

Mrs Morping played the piano and they sang a hymn called *Fight the Good Fight*. Miss Bell then told the pupils and staff how exciting it was for the school and for all the Barrowmarsh villagers to have their very own village football team, The Thursdays, playing in the first round of the FA Cup for the first time in the club's long and proud history.

'Humph,' Nails snorted. 'Football, football, football; I hate football.'

After assembly, Mr Frost's class had literacy. 'Brilliant,' said Jimmy, 'we're doing Poems with a Twist.' Everyone seemed to enjoy the lesson – all except Nails, that is, who claimed he couldn't find his book ... then his pen was missing ... then his chair was wobbly, then he needed to go to the toilet ... then he said he couldn't remember what it was they were supposed to be doing. Mr Frost found a book and a pen for Nails, and then just explained everything again.

Jenny whispered to Sam and Jimmy, 'Did you notice how patient Mr Frost was?'

Jimmy worked in a group with Sam and his teaching assistant, Megan, while Jenny worked with Yunara. They wrote lots of Poems with a Twist.

Jimmy whistled as he worked. 'How about this?' he said:

> Got the pitch,
> Got the teams,
> Got the nets,
> Got the crowd,
> But...
> No ball!

The others laughed at the poem but Sam shook his head. 'You can't play football without a ball.'

'You're right, Sam,' Megan smiled, 'and that's what makes the poem funny or interesting; it has a *twist* at the end.'

Sam frowned ... and then smiled. 'Can we do a poem about my badges?'

So, they got together and threw in a few ideas. 'Here we go,' said Jenny, smiling:

> Got the table,
> Got the bag,
> Got the album,

Got the badges,
But...
No Sam!

Sam smiled; he liked the poem, and Yunara chuckled as she started to jot down a few new ideas.

'It's lovely to see you smile, Sam,' Megan beamed, 'and great to see *you* laughing, too, Yunara.'

Yunara nodded. 'I like school work, and I like being in Barrowmarsh ... but I still miss Africa.'

Without looking up from his work, Sam said, 'Mr Frost told everyone, before you came, that we would have new children from Africa and that we had to look after you because there'd been a war in your country, and that you'd had a very difficult time.'

Everyone stopped and looked at Sam.

'Shall we get your topic book, Sam?' Megan said, quickly.

'Mr Frost told us,' Sam continued, 'that we should make you and your brother very welcome, just like we made Norman Nailsworthy welcome when he came to our school.'

Nails glared at Sam from across the table. 'I didn't want to come to this dead-end village!'

Yunara shrugged. 'Well, I like it here.'

'You didn't like it when you first came here.' Sam kept his eyes fixed on the table. 'You didn't laugh or smile or talk much.'

'Okay, Sam,' Megan interrupted. 'Maybe that's just a little too much information.' She moved round to sit next to him. Jenny looked at her brother and raised an eyebrow.

Yunara took a deep breath. 'I know, Sam, but we're used to everything now. Do you remember when we first arrived? You came over our house with Jenny and Jimmy to play with us, and that was good.'

Sam shrugged. 'You have cushions, curtains, pyjamas and a lampshade covered with wild animals and flowers ... and Jandir has Spiderman on everything.'

Yunara smiled. 'Harry and Kalisha, our foster parents, took us to Cardiff to choose lots of new things for our bedrooms.'

Megan laughed. 'Don't tell me – you have a room full of animals; you're animal crazy!'

Yunara's grin broadened. 'My room's not as bad as my brother's ... Spiderman clothes, toys and posters absolutely everywhere!'

Nails slammed a book onto the table and turned away. 'Take no notice,' Megan whispered as they all looked towards Nails.

Mr Frost quickly sat down next to the grumpy boy. 'Now then, Norman, let's have a look at all the good work you've been doing ...'

Yunara spread her fingers on the table and glanced at Jenny. 'I also have a Cath Kidston bag, purse and iPod case – and that's because of Jenny.'

Jenny grinned. 'I knew you'd like them.'

'Like them! – I bet you do!' said Megan. 'I adore Cath Kidston bags.'

Yunara nodded slowly. 'I love the patterns, but I really love animals. I want to be a vet when I grow up ... and look after sick animals in Africa.'

Jenny's eyes widened. 'That would be so awesome.'

'So what was it like in the part of Africa that you were from?' Jimmy asked. 'Did you have DVDs?'

'Of course we did,' Yunara laughed. 'We had a big, wide-screen television and a DVD player in our house, but we didn't have Spiderman.' She rolled her eyes and laughed again.

'Did you leave your home because of the war?' Sam asked, abruptly.

'Sam!' Jenny whispered, and Mr Frost turned and looked over the top of his reading glasses.

Yunara nodded slowly. 'Yes, Sam, we did. When the men in Jeeps arrived in our town we had to leave everything behind and go to another house, where we had nothing. When the men with guns came,' she continued, 'we had to move quickly, during the night, to a very small house in a strange town.'

All eyes were on Yunara. Even Nails had half turned and was clearly listening. 'Mama became very sick and was taken to a hospital across the wire fences, to a different country ...'

The room was in absolute silence; children on other tables had stopped what they'd been doing and were listening as Yunara quietly told her story.

'We didn't know where our Baba was ... he'd been at our house on the night we left, but by the next morning he wasn't with us.'

'Who's Baba?' Sam asked.

'Baba is my father. The word for mother in Swahili, our language, is Mama, and the word for father is Baba.'

Nails stood up and walked to the opposite end of the classroom.

'What happened next?' Sam asked.

Jenny knew from her chats with Yunara what came next, but she wondered if she would say in front of everyone.

'We were taken from the little house,' said Yunara, chewing her fingernail, 'to a camp full of tents and shelters made from old boxes and pieces of wood. I'm not sure how long we were there, but we were scared the whole time. We were looked after by a woman we didn't know, and lots of other children were very sick ... The thing I remember most, apart from missing Mama and Baba and wondering when they'd come for us, was being frightened ... I remember keeping Jandir under a net in a wooden shelter, and trying to keep him away from sick children and the disgusting smell. It smelt horrible all over the camp. The place was full of mosquitos. And people crying.'

Yunara paused, put her hands to her cheeks, and stared ahead.

'Are you okay, Yunara?' Mr Frost said, quietly.

She looked up, thought for a moment, and nodded.

The whole class had turned to face her, and Nails slouched against a windowsill with his head bowed.

Mr Frost looked around the room and shrugged. 'It seems we have things to talk about ... providing that's okay with you, of course, Yunara.'

She looked from the twins to the teacher and smiled.

'So,' said Mr Frost, 'does anyone have a question for Yunara?'

Someone asked, 'How did you get away from the camp?'

'I don't remember too much about it. I think we were taken in a lorry, but I remember waking up in a clean hospital with beds. We went on an aeroplane, and I kept thinking we would meet with Mama and Baba, but we stayed in a big house where we were looked after by nurses and doctors, and people who smiled and were kind, but asked lots of questions.'

'Were you in this country?' Jimmy asked.

'Yes,' Yunara replied. 'We met Harry and Kalisha, and after going out to lots of nice places with them we were asked if we'd like to live with them for a while. We told them we wanted to go back home to live with Mama and Baba, and Jandir cried all the time.'

Mr Frost walked round the table to Yunara. 'You're a brave girl, Yunara, and we all know how well you look after your brother.'

'There was a lady called Molly,' Yunara continued, 'who came to visit us at Harry and Kalisha's house. We asked when we'd be going home, and she told us that she couldn't promise anything, but she'd see what she could do. She said that we would hear the words 'asylum seeker' a lot, and that we could end up living with Harry and Kalisha for quite a long time.'

Jenny leaned back in her chair. 'Harry and Kalisha are really brilliant when we come over to visit.'

Yunara smiled.

'And,' Jenny added, 'Kalisha has taught us how to make African jewellery.'

The smile spread across Yunara's face. 'Kalisha came here from Africa too, when she was a little girl. She speaks Swahili, and we all spoke English and some

French in Africa. Harry speaks Welsh, and I'm learning some too.'

Her smile faded and she looked down at her hands. 'The hardest thing, though, is that Jandir keeps asking when we'll be seeing Mama and Baba again.'

The break-time bell rang. Mr Frost and Megan had a quiet chat with Yunara as everyone went out to play.

After Monday's Literacy session the class had Maths. They were doing division, which the twins found okay. Sam could do division really well, and multiplication, too, and he could do them together! Mr Frost said that it was the best way to understand them properly. He told the class that when you did them together it was called 'inverse operations'.

'I can do that,' Sam said, shyly, 'you just have to look at the patterns with the numbers.'

Sam could do Inverse Operations with lots of really big numbers, and he could do them in his head! When Mr Thomas, a school inspector, came to Barrowmarsh Primary, Sam followed him around for most of the day, saying, 'I've been learning about inverse operations. Ask me some questions, Mr Inspector Man. Ask me any number, the bigger the better ... Go on, ask me.' Mr Thomas asked Sam lots of questions, but soon ran out of questions because Sam could answer them all!

Jenny jotted in her Treasure Book that it must be brilliant to be like Sam and be cleverer than a school inspector! She also wrote about some of Sam's other ideas that Mr Frost called 'extremely interesting'. One day, their teacher said that it was time to clear up and that he didn't know where the time had gone. Sam asked Mr Frost where, exactly, *did* time go, and then asked if it would ever return! Mr Frost scratched his head and said, 'Wow!'

Near the end of the school day, Mr Frost told everyone to sit in their places for Circle Time and Signing Out.

Sam showed everyone the new badges he'd got from the World Wildlife Association. He was always happy to talk to his close friends but he didn't like having to face bigger groups of people. With Megan's help, he told the class about endangered species and about how important it was to help ensure they didn't become extinct like dinosaurs.

After Sam's talk, the others were invited to ask questions. Jenny was first. 'Did you write to The World Wildlife Association for information?'

Sam looked to Megan for reassurance. 'Yes, I wrote a letter and my dad helped me.'

Nails suddenly slammed his fist onto a table. 'Can't you do anything for yourself, daft boy?'

The classroom fell silent, shocked by Nails' angry outburst.

Sam stared at Nails, blankly. 'My name is Samuel John Foley, not daft boy.'

No one spoke or moved.

Mr Frost sat down next to Nails. 'So, would you like to talk about this?'

Nails kept his eyes lowered. His face was red and his fists clenched.

'I'm sure Sam is unhappy about your behaviour,

Norman,' Mr Frost said, calmly, 'but why are you so angry?'

Nails drummed the table with his fingers but said nothing.

Mr Frost gave him a few moments. 'Just think about it, Norman; think about why you reacted in that way, and think about how your actions make other people feel.' The teacher looked around the circle and asked, 'Does anyone else want to say anything?'

Slowly, Yunara put her hand in the air and said, 'I felt sad, too, when ...' She hesitated, 'I was upset and I wanted to go somewhere, alone, when ...' She took a deep breath, '... when Sam mentioned that his *dad* helped him ... but I wasn't angry.'

Nails darted a look at Yunara, then lowered his eyes.

Jenny glanced at her brother; she thought that, for just a moment at least, Nails actually looked sad.

Mr Frost nodded to Yunara, and then turned to Nails.

'Whenever you're ready, Norman ... I'll leave it up to you.' He then stood and said to the class, 'Okay guys, we have a little bit of time left, would anyone like to talk about anything else?'

Jimmy asked Mr Frost why Saturday's game against Northolme Nomads in the FA Cup was so important.

The teacher pondered for a moment. 'A good question, Jimmy, and I believe both Barrowmarsh and Northolme can feel extremely proud of reaching this stage of the FA Cup. It is such a prestigious ...' (another flurry in Jenny's bag) '... and world-famous cup competition.' Mr Frost rubbed his chin, and then continued, 'There are lots of early matches in the FA Cup where smaller teams, like Barrowmarsh and Northolme, have to play each other in order to qualify for the stage where professional teams come into the competition. We, of course, have successfully reached that stage of the FA Cup.'

He walked around with his hands in his pockets, smiling to himself and quietly saying over and over again, 'The FA Cup, first round ...'

'Ahem ...' He turned to the class, and blinked. 'However, we will be playing another small team, Northolme Nomads.'

'Does that mean we could beat them, Mr Frost?' Jimmy asked.

'Well Jimmy, we have a very good chance, but I'm sure Northolme will be desperate to win, too. And, like us, I'm sure they'll go into the match believing that they can win.'

Yunara put her hand up. 'What happens if we win, Mr Frost?'

'Ah, then, Yunara,' Mr Frost beamed, 'we'd move into the second-round of the FA Cup.'

'Yeah, yeah,' Nails sneered, 'or maybe we'd all wake up from this stupid dream.'

Mr Frost ignored the comment. 'Just think, everyone, if we beat Northolme and reach the next round, we could be drawn against a team such as Shrewsbury Town, Bristol Rovers or Coventry City ... now wouldn't that be something?'

Mr Frost lapsed into silence again and stood, gazing out of the window with a dreamy smile on his face ... 'and then it's the third round, and the chance of playing one of the really big teams ... Cardiff City, Swansea City, Chelsea, Arsenal ... or maybe, just maybe even ...'

The bell rang, dragging Mr Frost out of his daydream.

'Anyway, class, we have to overcome Northolme Nomads first. Get your things; make sure your tables are tidy and off you go ... see you all tomorrow.'

Chapter Four

Saturday arrived at last, and with it the FA Cup first round match. The team bus stood outside Druid's Lodge, its engine rumbling and the smell of diesel wafting around the forecourt, but inside the guest-house a crisis was unfolding ...

Jimmy stood back as Dad flew past. He could see that he was in a bit of a sweat. Dad couldn't find one of his football-boots and was rushing around, having a tizzy fit, moving things, throwing things and crawling under things. Jenny and Jimmy tried to help but Teabag thought it was a great game and rushed around, yapping wildly.

'They were here, both boots were right here.' Dad pointed to a single boot on one of the kitchen chairs, his outstretched finger trembling. 'But now there's only one; one boot, can you believe it!' The twins could see their dad was in a right state and tried to help by looking under all the kitchen chairs, under the table, in cupboards and even in the bins!

'When did you last see the *two* boots?' Mum asked, patiently.

'WHEN I CLEANED THEM LAST NIGHT,'

'Perhaps you only cleaned one, dear, and there's really no need to shout.' Mum was trying to be helpful, and was working even harder trying to stay calm.

Dad looked bemused. 'Why on earth would I have cleaned just one boot?'

'Well *I* don't know,' Mum shrugged, 'maybe it's your favourite kicking foot or something.'

Dad looked up to the ceiling and muttered something that the twins couldn't hear!

Outside, the coach driver revved the engine a couple of times, adding to the noise and sending clouds of diesel fumes into every part of Druid's Lodge.

'Come on, come on,' some of the players shouted from the bus. 'Get a move on boss, what's keeping you?' Other players started singing, 'Oh why are we waiting, why are we waiting?'

Dad darted through the entrance hall, past Jenny and Jimmy, nearly fell over Teabag, and ran outside.

'I'M LOOKING FOR MY MISSING BOOT, THAT'S WHY YOU LOT ARE WAITING!' He dashed back into house, ran through to the kitchen and started throwing things around again; he was really angry by this time!

Mum stood with her arms folded, tapping her foot and saying, through her teeth, 'Calm down, Jack, calm down!'

'I think Mum's going to explode in a minute,' Jenny hissed.

Mr Frost got off the coach to help look for the lost boot, and even Miss Bell decided to lend a hand, but there was no sign of it anywhere.

The twins stood in the kitchen, trying to keep an excited Teabag out of everyone's way. Everyone ran around doing what Jenny and Jimmy had already done, opening cupboards and drawers, looking under the table and chairs for the umpteenth time, and digging down into the re-cycling bins.

'There's only one thing for it, Jack,' Miss Bell said, after deciding the boot was well and truly lost, 'I'll go and see if any other player has a spare pair you can borrow.'

As she walked to the front door Teabag leapt from Jenny's arms, shot past her and ran out of the house. Miss Bell walked over to the bus, then stopped suddenly and pointed across the village green. Her voice rose to a high pitched squeal. '*That, that ... creature!*' She pulled a horrible face. '*That horrible, furry flea-bag of yours is digging up our beautiful village green.*'

Jimmy got a terrible sinking feeling.

All eyes turned to where Teabag was digging furiously, earth and grass flying everywhere!

'I really don't have time to worry about that scruffy mutt, or the village green.' Dad was exasperated. 'Now where on earth is my other boot?'

The twins looked at each other. 'Uh-oh!' The same thought had occurred to each of them and they ran across the grass in time to see Teabag using his front paws to pull loose dirt from a freshly-dug hole.

'TEABAG,' they called together. Their little dog leapt and bounced about as if he had springs on his paws. His tongue lolloped and his tail wagged in frenzied excitement.

Jimmy grabbed him and tickled him behind the ear. 'We haven't come to play.'

'What have you done, Teabag?' Jenny coaxed, smiling at him. She started scooping the loose earth and stones out of the newly dug pit. Teabag jumped from Jimmy's arms and bounced up and down, barking playfully. By this time, everyone had followed the twins onto The Green. Jimmy pushed his hand down into the soil and pulled out ... Dad's football boot, all muddy and grubby and full of earth!

'Aaaarghhh,' Dad wailed. 'That dog, I'll swing for 'im, the little ... The little ... PEST!'

Jenny covered her mouth and spluttered, as Mum patted Dad's shoulder. 'Now, now, dear, take a deep breath and calm yourself. That's not what you say when he sits on your lap at home. You call him your *little pumpkin* and you tickle him.'

'TICKLE HIM, TICKLE HIM?' Dad's face was very red and his voice high pitched and squeaky. 'I'LL DO MORE THAN TICKLE HIM WHEN I GET HOLD OF HIM!'

With Dad and his boots finally on the bus, Mr Frost, who had recovered sufficiently from his injured knee and had been declared fit to play, nodded to the driver.

The twins had grown up with the football team. They knew that Barrowmarsh Thursdays were used to playing matches in front of a handful of spectators. It was usual for them to take only one bus to an away game. This game would be no exception; the players and a few adult supporters travelled on the single coach. The twins' dad promised that, should the Thursdays reach the FA Cup second-round and have an away game, then an extra coach would be hired for villagers, and Druid's Lodge would close for the day. Jimmy kept his fingers crossed.

The twins and their mum shouted 'good luck' to everyone as the door closed with a whoosh and the coach pulled away. 'Look,' Jenny said, 'Miss Bell is walking up and down the bus counting everyone. I bet she's asking if anyone needs to visit the 'little boys' room' or 'little girls' room' before setting off!'

Jenny held onto Teabag as they waved to all the smiling faces on the bus. In the back window there was a huge banner. It had a big red dragon at the top and the words:

Mighty Thursdays, Wembley here we come!

And, in the middle there was a large FA Cup made out of silver paper by the children in the school's nursery.

Shortly after the bus had pulled away Jenny asked if she and Jimmy could go and play in the village playground. They knew that there would be no live coverage of the match on television or on the radio. They also knew they'd have to wait until the game ended for the sports results and final match report.

Mum nodded from behind a pile of fresh laundry. The Lodge was a family-run guest-house, and all members of the family helped in its day-to-day running, including Jimmy and Jenny. Earlier, they had put tea, coffee, sugar and biscuits in the rooms in readiness for guests. As Dad was away playing football, it was Mum's turn to be on duty for the day.

'We're going to call for Sam first, if that's okay, Mum?'
'Yes, that's fine,' she answered, 'but take Teabag with

you, and don't go further than the playground or Sam's house.'

The twins called for Sam and went to the playground where they met Yunara and Jandir, who were there with their foster parents. It was bitterly cold – the sort of day when the ends of fingers and toes, ears and noses tingle almost painfully – and they were all wrapped up in their coats, cosy hats and scarves; well, except for Teabag, of course, who was wrapped up in his teddy-bear coloured wool. The twins had researched poodles on the internet one day at school and had been surprised to find that they didn't have fur like most dogs but wool, like sheep!

The youngsters stamped their feet, clambered over the climbing frames, and ran around to keep warm, while Harry and Kalisha sat on a park bench with a flask of hot tea.

'Do you think Matthew Henderson, our mid-fielder, will want to play football on a day as cold as this?' Jimmy asked the others.

Jenny shrugged. 'He'll certainly have an attitude if he has to play today.'

Yunara said that it was never as cold as this in the part of Africa where they were from.

'Perhaps Matthew Henderson would prefer to play football in Africa,' Jimmy suggested,

Jenny thought about it. 'No, I don't think he would, he'd probably have an attitude about it being too warm!'

Harry and Kalisha chuckled but said nothing.

In the afternoon Jandir went off with Harry and Kalisha to visit family friends in Oswestry.

Arrangements had been made and Yunara was allowed to join Sam and the twins for the rest of the afternoon. They strolled across the village green and waved to Alison, the community police officer, who was on duty for the day. Martin, the other village policeman, was a forward for The Thursdays and was away with the team.

They sat on the stiff and crunchy grass near Druid's Pond, which was quite big and had a small island in the middle. Sometimes, they liked to make up stories about being marooned on the island, like Robinson Crusoe. Jenny remembered that their dad had thought it a great idea … 'It would give me some peace and quiet,' he'd said, 'especially if you took that pest of a mutt with you, too!'

Throughout the year ducks swam on the pond and waddled about the village green and the little central island. In warmer weather the twins and their friends liked to watch fish swimming close to the surface. Jimmy pointed out that parts of the pond were covered in thin ice. 'It's not frozen all over but the water must be very cold.'

'Grandad always says to be careful because the pond can be extremely dangerous,' Jenny warned.

Jimmy gave a mischievous smile. 'Yes, it's over a hundred metres deep with a ginormous octopus living at the bottom!'

Teabag wagged his tail.

'I don't like it,' Sam mumbled, nervously, 'can we move away please?'

Yunara looked a little unsure.

Jenny tutted. 'It isn't really a hundred metres deep, and *I've* never seen an octopus in it, so don't worry.'

'Just because *you* haven't seen one doesn't mean there isn't an octopus in there ...' Jimmy looked at Teabag ... 'a giant dog-eating octopus!'

Teabag wagged his tail.

'Ignore him, Sam,' Jenny said. 'Besides, an octopus wouldn't live in a pond, it's a sea creature.'

Yunara thought about this for a moment. 'I still think its deep enough to be dangerous, if you weren't careful or if you couldn't swim.'

Sam beamed. 'I can swim.'

'I know you can,' Jenny smiled, 'you're in the top group, with Yunara, when our class goes swimming on Wednesdays.'

Just then, they heard a familiar but not altogether welcome voice behind them ...

'If you're so clever, Sammy boy, why don't you swim across the pond to the island; show us that superior front-crawl technique that Frosty's always banging on about!'

It was Nails!

'I ... I can't swim across the p ... p ... pond,' Sam stammered, 'I don't have my trunks or a towel and my mum says that under no circumstances should I go into the pond.'

'Oooo, mummy's boy,' Nails mocked, before turning on Yunara. 'And what about you; have Mama and Baba warned you about the pond, too?'

Yunara clenched her fists but Jimmy stepped forward. 'Just leave it; he's not worth the trouble.'

Nails continued to press. 'Come on then, let's see the top group swim.'

'It's far too cold and dangerous, Norman,' Jenny said, hotly. 'And it's full of weeds, which could cause all sorts of problems.'

Nails sneered. 'Huh, scaredy cats!'

Jenny ignored his comment. 'Also, the water could be full of nasty germs.'

'And there's an octopus that eats dogs!' Sam glanced at the pond and took a step back.

Teabag wagged his tail.

Nails laughed loudly. 'Good! Go on, Sammy boy, I dare you to swim across, and take the scruffy pooch with you. You can't back out of a dare ... unless you're a weak, little coward.'

'Darers go first!' Jenny snapped.

Nails glared at them. 'But I double dare you, and if you don't do it, it'll prove that you're nothing but a snivelling, lily-livered scaredy-pants.'

'I'd rather not,' Sam said, quietly, chewing his thumb. 'My mum said I ...'

'Yeah, yeah,' Nails sneered. 'Mummy said ...'

Yunara took a few quick steps towards Nails. 'Stop saying that!'

Nails squared up to her. 'Oh it's you again, the new kid. Remind me ... Where, *exactly*, are your mother and father?'

Yunara turned away and Jimmy could see tears rolling down her face.

'*LEAVE HER ALONE,*' Jenny screamed.

Nails snarled and jabbed a finger into her shoulder. 'Who asked you?'

'We just want to be left alone, that's all.'

'So, Miss Clever Clogs wants to be left alone, does she?' Nails smirked and pushed Jenny.

'HEY, DON'T PUSH MY SISTER,' Jimmy yelled.

'I'll push whoever I like.' Nails sneered and moved slowly towards Jenny again, his eyes bulging and his teeth clenched.

Teabag crouched, stared at Nails and started to growl. The deep rumble grew louder and angrier.

Nails hesitated, which gave Teabag the opportunity to leap between him and Jenny. The dog bared his white teeth and kept growling; he edged forward, his front legs and shoulders lowered and hunched in readiness to pounce.

Nails backed away quickly. 'I ... I was only joking,' he stuttered, his eyes fixed on the small animal.

Teabag continued to growl threateningly as he edged towards the bully. Nails backed away hurriedly, but the courageous dog followed him, snarling and stalking, keeping pace with the boy.

They had moved a little way from the pond when Nails stumbled and fell awkwardly onto his back. Suddenly, Teabag pounced at the sprawling boy.

Jenny screamed. '*TEABAG!*'

Jimmy gasped.

Nails raised a hand in a desperate attempt to protect his face. Teabag bounded around his head, stopped, wagged his tail ... and licked Nails' face.

Yunara and Jenny threw back their heads and laughed, and Sam smiled.

Jimmy shouted, 'Teabag, come here, boy.'

The dog hesitated and raised his head for a moment

before turning his attention back to the bewildered bully. Teabag gave a little yap and licked Nails' face again.

'Come on, there's a good boy,' Jenny called, brightly. 'Good doggy.'

Teabag turned and bounded back to his owners, his tail wagging furiously.

Nails had disappeared so the group of friends decided to go up to Sam's house to see Kellogg, his pet corn-snake. Sam took Kellogg out of his warm, glass tank so that the twins and Yunara could hold him.

'This is so cool,' said Yunara, smiling broadly.

Jimmy teased Teabag. 'This is a dog-eating snake!'

Teabag wagged his tail.

Jenny and Yunara laughed but Sam bit his lower lip and looked from Kellogg to Teabag and back to Kellogg again.

They told Sam's mum what had happened with Nails down at the pond. She tutted, frowned and asked Yunara if she was all right. She said that Nails was a bully and that they should always try to steer well clear of him.

Jimmy scratched his head. '*Steer* clear of him?' He pondered this latest example of grown-ups saying strange things. He asked Jenny if Sam's mum was being sarcastic.

Jenny flicked through her Treasure Book. 'No, she was speaking *metaphorically*.'

'Wow, sis, I don't think I'm ever going to be able to learn all the crazy things you need to know to be a grown-up! I told Mum, once, that I wasn't ever going to grow up, and that I was going to stay a child all my life, and do you know what she said?'

'What did she say, bro?'

'She said that it was okay, because that's exactly what our father has managed to do!'

Jenny nodded, knowingly. 'I think Mum was being sarcastic!'

Once she'd been given the full story of the incident with Nails, Sam's mum told them that they should let an adult know, immediately, if he caused them any further problems. But she, too, smiled when she heard about Teabag pouncing on Nails and licking his face.

Sam's dad popped his head around the door and asked if the twins would like to stay for tea. 'We've already sorted it with Harry and Kalisha,' he added, 'Yunara is staying.'

They told him they'd love to, so he went to phone their mum to check that it would be okay.

A little while later everyone was called to the kitchen for tea. The radio was on, and as they sat around the table they were told that lots of match reports from the FA Cup first-round had started coming in. It was a quarter to five and most games were nearing full-time whistles.

Sam's dad, Mr Foley, poured tea and handed out some plates. 'We caught a brief report a little while back about our very own Barrowmarsh Thursdays.'

'How are they doing?' Jimmy asked, excitedly.

'Well,' he grinned, 'there were about ten minutes left to play and we were leading one-nil. Can you believe it?'

'Yes,' Sam said, seriously, 'I *can* believe it because you just told us, and it was on the radio.'

'Let's hope we can hold on.' Jenny crossed her fingers.

They listened to the radio as they had tea ... Brentford were still ahead in their game, Newport County had been victorious in an earlier kick-off, while Wrexham and Rochdale were still level ...

The radio presenter babbled on; more and more results were coming through.

'Come on, come on,' Sam's mum urged, 'what about The Thursdays?'

'And now,' the announcer said crisply, 'the final whistle has just blown at ...' they all held their breath ... but it was not the Northolme versus Barrowmarsh game. They all groaned, and the report seemed to go on forever. More results were announced ... and then came the words that made everyone stop eating ...

'Okay,' said the presenter, 'we can now go over to Northolme, where the home team, The Nomads, have been playing the Welsh Borders League side, Barrowmarsh Thursdays ...'

There was a crackle ... silence, then another series of crackles!

'Oh for goodness sake,' Mr Foley grumbled, 'why doesn't someone sort it out?'

'Hush, Phil,' his wife hissed, as the radio crackled back into life and a voice drifted from the box ... 'Hello? Hello Bob, can you hear me?'

'Yes, we can hear you,' the presenter confirmed. 'Go ahead with your report.' Jimmy, desperate for the toilet, hopped about – he couldn't miss this!

'Well, Bob,' the reporter continued, 'the referee has

just blown his whistle to end the game and I can tell you that we've had some late, high-drama here at Northolme ...'

'Get on with it,' Sam's dad muttered, irritably, 'what was the score?'

Jimmy looked at Jenny, who now had the fingers of both hands crossed.

'The first half,' said the reporter, 'was a pretty dour affair with neither team dominating the game, and both sets of players looking extremely nervous ... The Northolme manager must have had a few strong words at half-time because his players came out for the second half like a team possessed and threw the kitchen sink at Barrowmarsh ...'

Sam frowned and looked at the radio.

Jimmy and Yunara chuckled.

'Shush,' Mrs Foley said, putting a finger to her lips.

' ... Geraint Morgan, the Barrowmarsh goalkeeper, pulled off a series of spectacular saves, and Jack Jones ...'

'*THAT'S OUR DAD!*' Jenny shrieked.

'Shushhh,' they all hissed.

'... the Thursdays' centre back, cleared an almost certain goal off the line with his keeper stranded!'

'YESSSS!' the twins yelled. 'Well done, Dad!'

The reporter's voice droned on. 'Then, after Northolme had hit the post twice and the crossbar once, Barrowmarsh broke away in a swift and flowing counter-attack, and, miraculously, and against the run of play, took the lead with a spectacular, twenty five metre shot from veteran midfielder, Freddy Frost!'

'YAYYYYY!' They all jumped out of their seats.

Sam frowned again and looked from Jimmy to Jenny. 'But our teacher is called MISTER Frost, not Freddy.'

'That's right, Sam,' Jimmy told him, 'but he's also called Freddy ... and he scored for The Thursdays, brilliant!'

A smile spread across Sam's face. 'Yes, I like Mr Frost; he lets me show everyone my badges in Circle Time.'

'But then, drama,' the radio commentator said. 'With just two minutes of the match left disaster struck for brave Barrowmarsh!'

The dancing stopped, suddenly, and they all slumped down in stunned silence, as the commentator said: 'Benson, the tricky Northolme winger, waltzed through the bedraggled Barrowmarsh defence only to be brought down with a clumsy tackle in the area by centre-back, Jones.'

'*WHAT? DAD!*' Jimmy shrieked. '*What were you thinking of?*'

Mr Foley turned up the volume on the radio as the report continued: 'The referee had no hesitation in pointing to the penalty spot, and the Barrowmarsh player-manager was shown a yellow card.'

'Lucky he didn't get a red card,' Mrs Foley whispered, and Jenny agreed.

The radio crackled but the reporter's voice was still there. 'O'Leary, for Northolme, stepped up and gave goalkeeper, Geraint Morgan, no chance as he smashed the ball into the roof of the net for a Northolme equaliser.'

'Oh no,' Jenny muttered, glumly, staring down at her hands.

The radio commentator was still in full flow as he described how the crowd at Northolme had gone wild with joy, ecstatic at getting an equaliser. The twins, Yunara, Sam and his parents listened quietly, as the reporter added, 'The game moved into four minutes of injury time ... and *then*,' he paused, dramatically, 'came the final twist!'

They all looked at each other, terrified at what they might hear. 'Oh please,' Jenny groaned, 'not another Northolme goal.'

'And then,' the announcer said, again, for effect, 'with only twenty-five seconds left on the clock, and with both sets of supporters settling for a draw, Barrowmarsh mid-fielder, Sahidol Ali, launched the ball up-field. The substitute, Matthew Henderson, controlled it beautifully on his chest, slipped it cleverly past a defender and darted into the Northolme area. The goalkeeper charged out and two big defenders closed in but Henderson kept his cool to steer the ball past the lunging keeper and into the bottom corner of the net ... final score, Northolme Nomads, *one*, Barrowmarsh Thursdays, *two*.'

No one in the kitchen heard anything else from the radio. They leapt out of their seats and danced around, laughing, yelling and singing.

Teabag bounced up and down, barking, wagging his tail and doing his smiley face!

Sam stood still and grinned. 'Mr Frost's name is Freddy!'

Chapter Five

Another Monday morning, and the first day back at school after The Thursdays' brilliant FA Cup victory over Northolme Nomads. There was great excitement at Ysgol Gynradd Cors-y-domen, and everyone was eager to offer Mr Frost their congratulations for his spectacular goal and for his team's magnificent performance.

He grinned. 'Not sure I agree with being described as a veteran midfielder, though.' Everyone could see that he was delighted with the situation, and with all the praise that was coming the way of Barrowmarsh Thursdays Football Club.

Miss Bell was in top form during assembly, singing heartily and making constant references to the team's 'historic achievement' in reaching the second round of the most famous cup competition in the whole world!

Jimmy and Jenny sat with Sam and Yunara. Sam fidgeted with the bottom of his sweatshirt and kept looking to his side. Jimmy knew that it was because Nails was sitting just a few feet away. Every so often Nails turned and glared at them, and when Miss Bell spoke about Saturday's match he muttered things, quite loudly, like, 'Huh, football again! A team of deadbeats scrape a win against another team of deadbeats, big deal!'

After assembly the class sat on the carpet for News Time.

'Listen in, guys,' Mr Frost clapped his hands and smiled, 'let's find out some of the exciting things you got up to over the weekend. Now, who's going to start us off? Sam, what about you, what news do you have for us?'

Everyone looked at Sam, who looked down at the carpet. Mr Frost waited quietly and patiently for him to think of something to tell the class. Megan smiled and whispered some encouragement. 'Just take your time, Sam.'

Jimmy assumed he'd talk about his badges, but he didn't!

'On Saturday, at exactly 2:47 pm,' Sam began, quietly, 'Nails dared me to swim across Druid's Pond. I didn't want to and he made fun of me. He was nasty to Yunara about her mother and father, and he also picked on Jenny but Teabag scared him away ... Teabag growled a lot and Nails was frightened ... but Teabag only licked his face.'

For a few moments the class was as quiet as snow at midnight, but then Nails muttered, 'I was only joking. I didn't think you'd be stupid enough to take me seriously ... and I wasn't scared of that pathetic little pooch, he's just a ...'

Jenny snapped. 'Don't call Sam stupid, and Teabag isn't pathetic.'

Jimmy joined in; he remembered that Grandad had told him and Jenny that they should always stand up to bullies. 'You *were* scared of Teabag, even though he was kind to you in the end, and you weren't joking about the dare. You were being nasty and trying to bully Sam ... and you were really cruel to Yunara.'

Jenny added, 'Yes, you were so spiteful and hurtful to Yunara; you have absolutely no idea what she and Jandir have been through ...'

'YES, I DO ... WHY DOESN'T ANYBODY EVER ...?' Nails stopped suddenly and clenched his eyes shut.

Jimmy took a sharp breath. Jenny stiffened. Sam blinked, and Yunara's mouth fell open. Their eyes darted from Nails to their teacher.

Mr Frost, who had been listening carefully, walked over to Nails. 'Okay, Norman, I think we need to talk about this.' He waited for a few moments. 'Is it true, Norman? Did you say those things?'

No one dared breathe.

'Well?' Mr Frost asked again, 'Is it true, Norman?'

'*No way*, don't listen to them ... trouble is, they can't take a joke.'

Mr Frost stared at him for a few seconds; the class watched in silence. 'I'm prepared to listen to your account of what happened and I'll be happy to hear about how you and the others feel about things, but bullying, Norman, is no joke.'

The expression on Nails' face changed from a scowl to lip-curling anger. His red eyes moistened and his shoulders slumped. Then he looked up. His jaw was clenched and his nostrils flared, but he made no reply.

'Bullying is totally unacceptable. Do I make myself absolutely clear, Norman?'

'Hummmph,' Nails mumbled. His head drooped.

'I'm sorry Norman, I didn't quite hear your reply. Do I make myself crystal clear?'

'Humm, er ... suppose so ... yes,'

'Thank you.'

Jimmy breathed out, and slackened his grip on the sides of his chair.

Mr Frost looked at Yunara and the rest of the class, and put his hand on Nails' shoulder. 'What did you mean a few moments ago, Norman? Would you like to talk?'

Nails sighed, looked towards the floor and with his voice barely above a whisper, said, 'No ... I don't want to talk.'

'Well. When you do, I'm here to listen ... we're all here to help.'

Jimmy, Yunara and Jenny looked at each other. They were all thinking about what Nails had said when their teacher stood, clapped his hands and raised his eyebrows. 'Okay, guys, let's carry on with News-time.'

Jenny looked up and grinned. 'And so, what about you, Mr Frost, did you do anything exciting over the weekend?'

He scratched his head. 'Well now, let me see, I washed my car on Sunday, marked some Maths homework, watched a bit of television ... I can't quite remember anything else ... Oh yes, almost forgot.' He blushed. 'I scored the best goal ever seen in the entire history of the planet ... and in the FA Cup, too!'

The class shrieked with laughter and Mr Frost laughed more than any of them.

Later that morning, during play-time, Nails was careful to avoid the twins, Sam and Yunara. They watched from the other side of the playground as he sulked and shuffled around the yard on his own, his hands in his pockets and his shoulders hunched even more than usual.

'Do you know,' Jenny said, quietly, 'I actually feel sorry for him'

'Yeah, I know what you mean, sis. He must be very sad and lonely.'

After lunch, Mr Frost walked slowly into the classroom, his head lowered and his fingers pressed to his lips. He didn't seem to have his usual *bounce*.

'What's up with him?' Jimmy asked Jenny.

Their teacher stopped in front of the white-board and clapped his hands. 'Listen in, guys.' The class gathered around. 'Miss Bell and I have just been listening to the draw for the second round of the FA Cup.'

'Who will The Thursdays be playing, Mr Frost?' Yunara's eyes were wide.

'Well,' he hesitated for a few moments, 'there's good news and maybe not such good news ...'

Everyone stared at him; even Nails was quiet and appeared to be listening.

Mr Frost thought for a moment. 'We have a home game, which is good, but it's against Llanpowys Casuals, from our very own league.'

'So what's the bad news?' Jenny tilted her head to one side.

'I suppose we should be grateful, Jennifer,' Mr Frost ran his hand through his dark but greying hair, 'but we were all hoping to play a big, professional team from the Football League.'

'You'd be slaughtered if you did,' Nails muttered, quietly, flicking a pencil across the table.

Mr Frost ignored the comment. 'Perhaps we should

be thankful; we've played Llanpowys twice this season, and have drawn both games. So, I'm pretty sure we have a fair chance of beating them.'

'There's also a fair chance of losing to this other team of no-hopers,' Nails mumbled to himself, but loud enough for everyone to hear. 'And then maybe I wouldn't have to think about football at all.'

Mr Frost smiled and looked at Nails. 'Think positively, that's what I always say, Norman ... the glass is half full, not half empty! We can beat Llanpowys, and when we do we'll be in the dizzy heights of the FA Cup, third-round, along with ...' He stared into the distance, lost in a cloud of thoughts; a little smile on his lips, 'with Championship and ... and Premiership giants.'

Sam tugged at his sweatshirt, looked around quickly, and moved closer to Megan. 'I hope we don't have to play against giants, Mr Frost. I wouldn't like to see giants playing football against our team.'

Nails sniggered but Jenny glared at him, and so did Yunara.

Mr Frost coughed and turned to the class. 'I'm so sorry, Sam, I didn't make myself clear. I meant that teams like Everton, Swansea, Liverpool and Cardiff are very big and famous clubs; the players are ordinary men – very talented men, mind you, but ordinary men, so there's not too much to worry about!' He grinned and drifted into his dream-world again ... 'And the players of Llanpowys are ordinary men, too. It's just eleven players against eleven ordinary men. We *can* win ... we *will* win against Llanpowys Casuals!'

Jimmy grinned at Jenny and Yunara, and they smiled.

The week slid by and Wednesday was 'swimming day' for the twins' class. A bus picked them up outside the school where Megan counted everyone as they boarded the coach. Mr Frost checked to make sure they all had their swimming kits and towels.

Sam had learned to swim without armbands during the previous term and now his mum and dad took him to the pool every week so that he could practise. The twins knew that he could swim very well, but noticed that he still didn't like going from the changing room to the pool. He didn't like seeing lots of people in the water, and he really hated the noise and echoes of the pool. If there were people in the water, Sam would insist on walking in backwards so that he couldn't see them. Megan always helped him and he would put his hands over his ears until he got to the pool-side. Once he was in the water he was fine and got on with swimming.

Yunara also liked going to the pool; she told the twins that it was her favourite part of the week. She could swim, but she had never been to a swimming pool in her own country. A few people in the class thought everyone in Africa lived in huts. Yunara laughed and told them that Africa was huge, with lots of countries, and lots of different places and environments. She reminded them there were big, modern towns in the country where she and Jandir had lived with their parents, but the children of their town still liked to swim in the river, which was nice and warm but muddy and toffee-coloured.

Jenny remembered Yunara saying that everyone had to be careful when men with guns came to the river to get water. When they did, Yunara explained to a hushed class, the children would splash hurriedly to the far bank and hide amongst the trees and bushes until the men had filled their big cans and driven away.

There were no such problems in the Leisure Centre. Yunara now had a Cath Kidston swimming costume and a matching towel, but often said that she would be happier to be swimming in the big, warm river in Africa and living with Mama and Baba.

The bus dropped the class off at the swimming pool and they made their way through the foyer to the changing area. 'Look!' said Jenny, tapping her brother's shoulder. Mr Frost was talking to Nails, who had his hands in his pockets and was looking his usual, grumpy self.

'Really, Norman,' Mr Frost was saying, quietly, 'you can't keep on making excuses to get out of swimming. Is there something you'd like to talk to me about?'

Nails scowled and shook his head.

The twins and their friends hovered nearby and overheard Mr Frost say, 'Well, we'll have a quiet chat before next week, I'm sure we can sort things out. Let's just get into the pool, relax and have some fun.'

'Has Nails forgotten his swimming trunks?' Sam asked.

Mr Frost ushered everyone away from Nails. 'No, Sam, just a little misunderstanding, that's all. Nothing for us to worry about ... in you go, everyone, as quick as you can, please.'

'I don't think Nails can swim,' Jimmy whispered. 'Do you think I should tell Mr Frost?'

Jenny glanced over her shoulder. 'Mr Frost already knows he can't swim. He's just ... just ...' she flicked through her Treasure Book. 'He's just *preserving Nails' dignity.*'

'He's doing what?' Yunara asked.

Jenny repeated it, quietly.

'Who's preserving dignity, Jenny?' Mr Frost had overheard Jenny's last comment.

'Eh, hum, I was speaking ...' – another frantic flick through her Treasure Book – '... uh, hypothetically, Mr Frost.' Jenny blushed furiously.

The teacher grinned. 'I'm impressed, Jennifer. Okay guys, let's look sharp and get changed.'

'Hey sis, why did you say you were speaking pathetically?'

'Not pathetically,' she tutted, 'hypothetically!'

'What's that supposed to mean?'

Jenny thought for a few moments. 'It's a sort of imaginary for instance!'

'Well, why didn't you just say so?' Her brother grinned.

Everyone changed, got into their groups and slipped into the water. Nails, Jimmy noticed, walked slowly towards the shallow end by himself.

'Come along, Norman,' Mr Frost called, encouragingly, 'would you like one of the floats to start off with?'

Nails ignored him and continued to trudge back and

forth, along the edge of the pool. Everyone stared, but no one said a word.

Then, Sam waded over to where Nails stood. 'I couldn't swim when I first came here but Megan said I should try, persevere, and most of all, I should *believe*.'

'Why don't you push off, Dumbo.'

'My name isn't Dumbo. I've told you, it is Samuel John Foley!'

'Whatever!' Nails snapped, His face tightened and he poked his tongue into his cheek. Megan guided Sam back to his group.

Mr Frost spent the rest of the session with Nails, getting him to use a float and to lift one foot then the other off the pool floor. 'That's the ticket, Norman,' he coaxed, 'you're doing marvellously.'

Nails was the last one to shower, dry and change; he didn't want to be with anyone else. The twins and the rest of the class were waiting in the foyer and Megan was counting them again.

'Listen in, everyone.' Mr Frost called them together and he glanced towards the changing room door. 'When Norman comes out please act normally and don't make fun of him. We all have to learn new things in life, and we all have to start at the beginning at some point in our lives. That's the way it is at the moment with Norman and swimming.'

Jimmy scowled. 'Why shouldn't we make fun? He'd make fun of us.'

Mr Frost sighed. 'But do you *want* to be like that, Jimmy?'

Jimmy mumbled, apologetically. 'No, Mr Frost.'

'Would any of you want to be like Norman when he's being spiteful?'

They all shook their heads.

'I wonder what you'd think of yourselves if you were spiteful to others.'

'I wouldn't feel happy with myself,' Yunara murmured, and everyone agreed, nodding.

Megan smiled.

Mr Frost beamed. 'Thank you, guys, I knew you'd understand.'

Chapter Six

On Thursday, the class topic was 'dinosaurs' and Yunara asked Mr Frost how they had died out. Jenny reminded the class that the word 'extinct' could be used.

'That's right, Jennifer,' Mr Frost confirmed, 'dinosaurs are extinct, but we don't really know the reason for their extinction. History and pre-history is largely based on evidence, and we don't have enough evidence to know exactly why or how they died out.'

Sam whispered something to Megan, 'Tell the class,' she coaxed.

Sam looked down, tugged his sleeve, and said, 'Lots of large meteors hit the Earth, and damaged or polluted the atmosphere or caused drastic climate change that affected plant and animal life.'

Mr Frost nodded. 'Good theory, Sam.'

The twins and their friends often talked about things like that in Circle Time and in the playground too, especially if it was about dinosaurs.

Jimmy remembered that one of their favourite games was to pretend to hide from a ferocious Tyrannosaurus Rex that was skulking through Barrowmarsh looking for his dinner. Yunara didn't like playing hiding games because it scared her and reminded her of having to move from her home and hide from the men with guns.

Sam loved to find information, and with Megan's encouragement he told the class that some dinosaurs were carnivores and ate meat.

Jenny was always amazed that Sam didn't need a Treasure Book; he kept all his information in his head.

Sam wanted to say more to the class; he closed his eyes so he couldn't see anyone, and with Megan sitting next to him he told everyone that Kellogg, his corn snake, was a carnivore, and added that some dinosaurs were herbivores and only ate plants.

Jimmy was keen to ask a question. 'Mr Frost, I like to eat meat and apples, tomatoes and bananas, so does that mean I'm an omnivore?'

'Spot on, well done, Jimmy.'

Jimmy grinned. 'Our dad says that I'm a burgervore and Jenny is a chocovore!'

Everyone laughed and started making up new words for themselves and their eating habits.

Mr Frost stroked his chin. 'That's not a bad idea for homework, you could write a new description for the eating habits of all the members of your family.'

'What do you think you are, Mr Frost?' Jenny giggled.

'Well now, let me see,' he pondered, scratching his head. 'I know, I can honestly say that I'm a Tikka Massalavore!'

A lot of laughter was followed by a wave of excited chatter sweeping around the room, until Mr Frost clapped his hands and brought everything together. 'Okay guys, back to the plot, and dinosaurs! It is probable that some creatures that are alive today are descended from dinosaurs, like birds, crocodiles and snakes, for example.'

'Yes,' Jenny remarked, 'those creatures lay eggs, just like dinosaurs, and are not mammals.'

'Absolutely right, Jenny, and can anyone tell me anything about mammals?'

Sam whispered to Megan and she gestured for him to put his hand up.

Mr Frost nodded. 'Go on, Sam.'

Sam put his hands over his eyes. 'Human beings, cats, dogs and monkeys are mammals; the babies are born from their mums and don't hatch out of eggs ... And, shall I tell you something else that has nothing to do with mammals but is very, very interesting?'

Mr Frost leaned forward. 'Yes please, Sam, that would be great.'

'Well, cockroaches, which are beetly, insecty things, were around at the time of dinosaurs and are still around today! Not the very same ones, but their descendants.'

Mr Frost wrote a few notes on the white-board and asked the class to get out their project books and to carry on with their research. Jenny wrote 'descendants' in her Treasure Book, and Yunara was keen to find out about cockroaches

Jimmy chewed on a pencil as he worked. 'It's a pity that all the big dinosaurs are extinct, I think I'd like to see some of them in the fields around Barrowmarsh, well, the herbivores anyway. It would be great to see them chewing the leaves off tall trees and stretching their long necks over the hedges and fences so that we could tickle them under their chins.'

'I think Teabag would bark at them,' Jenny replied. 'He always barks at the magpies in our back garden and tries to chase them.'

'You're right, sis, and he barks at animals on

television. If horses, dogs or elephants are on the screen Teabag barks!'

Jenny chuckled. 'I like it when he barks whenever there's a scrum in a rugby match; he doesn't bother with the rest of the game but always barks at a scrum. Mum says it's because a scrum looks like a giant spider!'

The twins were still talking about dinosaurs when they were having tea with Mum and Dad that evening.

'I think they're extinct,' Jimmy said, 'because there weren't any vets sixty five million years ago, so when they became sick there was no one to give them tablets, pre-meds, operations and other things to make them better.'

Dad raised an eyebrow and said that it was probably a good thing. 'It's bad enough with Teabag, imagine the vet's bill if you owned a forty foot dinosaur!'

The weekend drew closer, and on the Friday evening, the night before the match against Llanpowys Casuals. Dad was giving his team-talk to the Barrowmarsh players in the family lounge of Druid's Lodge. Jimmy and Jenny loved to listen, and sometimes, when Dad used words such as 'commitment' and 'determination', Jenny would write them into her Treasure Book. He often used the word *hwyl*. The twins didn't really know what it meant but whenever Dad said, 'Show some *hwyl* and we can beat anyone,' all the players would shout and growl and thump the table! Whatever it was, the twins thought, *hwyl* sounded pretty scary!

During the team-talk on that Friday evening, Jimmy's ears pricked up when he heard their Dad warning the players about arguing.

'You must never argue with other players, and you must absolutely never argue with the referee ... you must show discipline at all times!'

'What?' Jimmy thought. 'I've heard *him* arguing with Mum!' The last time, he remembered, it happened just like this ...

'Jack, did you pick up the dog food from the shop?'

'What dog food?'

Mum sighed. 'The dog food to feed our dog, you know, that woolly little creature you may have noticed living in this house?'

Jenny said that Mum was being sarcastic!

'How was I supposed to know I was meant to get dog food? I'm not a mind-reader, you know!'

'JACK!' Mum was getting cross. 'I told you this morning that we needed dog food!'

'No, you didn't.'

'Yes, Jack, I did.'

'NO, you didn't!'

'YES, I DID!'

'NO, YOU ...'

'I DID, I DID, *I DID*!'

Jenny looked in her Treasure Book and announced that Mum was getting 'agitated'.

'JACK, sometimes I could scream. I'm sure you don't listen to a word I say. Your head is full of football, football, football!' Then she turned around, looked at the wall and folded her arms. Dad squished his eyebrows together and tugged his ear.

Mum stamped her foot and made a very loud sighing noise, which sounded like, 'HUFFFFF.'

And then, to Jimmy's amazement, Dad sneaked up behind Mum and TICKLED her!

Mum laughed and said, 'Jack, stop it!' Then he tickled her some more and she laughed even louder.

Then, and Jimmy shook his head in disbelief as he remembered it, Dad said, 'I love it when you're angry.' Then they CUDDLED!

Jimmy was absolutely certain that he didn't love it when Mum was angry. 'When Mum is angry it's time for me to scarper! I really, *really* don't understand grown-ups!'

The twins listened as Dad finished his team-talk. The meeting ended and everything was ready for Saturday's match.

Another week had slipped by and Saturday came around again, bringing with it the all-important FA Cup second-round match between Barrowmarsh Thursdays and Llanpowys Casuals. A lot more people than usual crowded around the fence that bordered the Parc y Derwydd football field. The referee looked around and checked that everything was in place. The assistant referees tugged at the nets to make sure there were no holes that would let the ball through, and then waved to the referee that all was well. The gleaming white ball had been placed on the centre spot ready for kick-off, and the players of both teams stood in their positions eager for the start. To the right, the village end, the Llanpowys players, in an all-blue kit, waited for the ref's whistle. To the left, the river end, Barrowmarsh Thursdays, in their white shirts, black shorts and white socks looked determined.

Mr Frost clapped his hands and shouted, 'Here we go

lads; for your families, for your friends ... for BARROWMARSH!'

Jimmy felt the usual rush of excitement as he waited for the sound of the whistle that would get ninety minutes of action, thrills, joy or misery underway.

Everyone cheered; the referee glanced at his watch, blew a long piercing blast and the game began.

The twins stood with Sam, Yunara and Jandir.

Jimmy heard Mum shout, 'Go on, Jack,' as Dad won a crunching tackle and cleared the ball up-field.

Everyone leaned forward as Mr Frost hit a ferocious, first-time shot. The Llanpowys goalkeeper was at full stretch and appeared to be well beaten as he dived despairingly to his right, but the ball crashed off the post and was bundled behind by a defender ... Corner to Barrowmarsh.

The twins started clapping and chanting, 'Barrowmarsh, Barrowmarsh, Barrowmarsh,' and laughed as Mr Braine, the 'Sarcastic Clapper', joined in with them.

The opposition's goalkeeper gathered the ball safely from the corner and cleared the danger. But, for the next twenty minutes it was all Barrowmarsh. The forwards were on fire! There were several shots at goal, and countless corner-kicks as the home-team piled on the pressure. Barrowmarsh went close and headers were cleared off the goal-line by desperate and overworked Llanpowys defenders. The home supporters cheered and clapped every kick.

'KEEP IT UP, THURSDAYS,' Grandad yelled, 'WE'VE GOT 'EM WORRIED.'

Jenny nudged her brother and laughed as Grandma scolded. 'Not so loud, Ernest, if you don't mind ... You're giving me a headache!'

Jimmy looked to see Grandad's reaction and grinned as he turned, winked at the twins and put his thumbs up.

Half-time came, and although Barrowmarsh had totally outplayed Llanpowys Casuals, there was no score. Miss Bell got up out of her chair near the half-way line and applauded loudly as the players trooped off the pitch for a well-deserved break.

Jimmy shook his head as he looked at their headmistress's chair. It was a special, high-backed wooden armchair that Mr Horton, the school caretaker, brought down to the pitch for every home game. Everyone called it The Throne!

'WELL DONE LADS, THAT'S THE SPIRIT, VERY WELL DONE,' Miss Bell boomed. 'KEEP IT UP; THEY'RE THERE FOR THE TAKING. WE CAN WIN THIS ONE!'

Everyone clapped as the players trudged off to Druid's Lodge for the half-time interval.

The sun was shining but it was cold and frosty and when the twins and their friends chatted big clouds of vapour came from their mouths.

Jimmy suggested a game. 'Let's pretend we're dragons and we're breathing fiery smoke. Let's see who can do the biggest dragon-smoke.'

They all puffed, and made roaring noises. Yunara couldn't roar because she was laughing too much. Grandad joined in their game, but Grandma, who was having a cup of tea from a flask said, 'For goodness sake, Ernest, be careful your teeth don't fall out!' This made Yunara laugh even more!

Mr Horton and John, the school lollipop-man, were selling raffle tickets to raise money for the football club. The prizes were a huge cake that Mrs Morping had baked, a black and white Barrowmarsh scarf made by the knitting club in Mr Frost's class, and a ride around the countryside and mountains on the back of Miss Bell's Hog!

'Can we get some tickets, please, Grandad?' Jenny asked.

'Of course we can.' He grinned, then turned and tapped Grandma's shoulder. 'Hey, Beattie, how about getting some tickets; you'd look a treat in a crash helmet and leather jacket, riding on the back of the Hog as one of Nell's Angels!'

'No thank you very much, Ernest, you won't catch me on the back of that dreadful contraption!'

Jenny whipped out her Treasure Book and dictionary, muttering, 'Contraption, contraption,' and Grandad hooted with laughter.

'COME ON YOU THUR-UR-UR URS-DAAAAAYS,' Miss Bell sang at the top of her voice as the players re-appeared from Druid's Lodge for the second half.

Llanpowys kicked off and went straight into a rare attack. Their strikers were covered and then tackled by the home team's full-backs. The ball spun to their left-winger, who hit a stinging shot through a crowd of defenders, only to see Geraint Morgan, the Barrowmarsh goalie, pull off a smart save.

Soon, the game settled to the pattern of the first half. The Thursdays' defence looked solid, and their midfielders kept good possession. Mr Frost was awesome, Jimmy thought, as he sprayed passes with ease to the busy forwards. Shots skimmed just wide of the Llanpowys goal and three efforts hit the woodwork. The Llanpowys goalkeeper was playing the game of his life, saving to his right and left, and diving bravely at the feet of rampaging Barrowmarsh forwards.

'ALL WE ARE SAY-ING,' the youngsters sang, 'IS GIVE US A GOAL!' Once again, Mr Braine joined in with the song, much to everyone's amusement.

Then, with only five minutes of the game left, Joe Rogers, the Barrowmarsh striker, was tripped just outside the Llanpowys penalty area. The referee immediately blew his whistle to signal a free kick. A wall of blue-clad players formed in front of the ball, and the referee marched them back, measuring out ten metres with his strides.

'COME ON THURSDAYS.' Jimmy urged the team on as he watched Mr Frost, Dylan Milkwood and Dad standing over the ball, talking. This was something they usually did whenever The Thursdays were awarded a free-kick.

Miss Bell was out of her Throne and was standing on the touchline. 'Make it count, Barrowmarsh, make it count!'

The players were ready and the referee blew a short, shrill note. Mr Frost ran towards the ball but jumped over it, tricking the defenders. Dad tapped it to his left, allowing Matthew Henderson to smash the shot goalward. The Llanpowys keeper didn't even see it, and the ball thundered into the back of the net!

'YEEEEEEEEEEESSSSSSSSSS.'

Jimmy jumped up and down, waving his black and white scarf while Jenny danced with glee. Yunara and Jandir bounced about, singing and laughing and Sam stood still but smiled. The hundred or so spectators clapped and whistled wildly, and broad grins spread across their faces.

Out on the pitch, just a few metres away, white shirted players ran and piled onto the team's number six.

Miss Bell's voice cut through the cheering and clapping. 'THAT'S THE STYLE, YOUNG HENDERSON, THAT'S THE STYLE!' She stood just over the touchline, on the playing field. 'THAT SHOULD DO IT; JUST THE TICKET. THERE ARE ONLY A FEW MINUTES LEFT, THEY WON'T COME BACK NOW!'

She strutted about the pitch, calling out instructions to individual players. 'Keep it tight, lads; when we re-start just run the clock down. Make sure you close them down. Are you listening to me Frederick? JUST CLOSE THEM DOWN!'

Everyone roared with laughter at the antics of the small, grey-haired headmistress, dressed in her usual tweed suit, shawl, huge, woolly match-day scarf and rosette.

The Barrowmarsh players had moved back into their own half, shaking hands and slapping backs, whilst the blue-shirted Llanpowys players, shoulders slumped and heads down, dejectedly, prepared to kick-off to re-start the game.

Miss Bell took a deep breath and cupped her hands to her mouth. 'MR FROST ... MR FROST, WATCH THEIR NUMBER EIGHT; KEEP ON HIS LEFT SIDE ... PUSH HIM WIDE!'

The red-faced referee ran across the field to the yelling headmistress, ready, no doubt, to give her a piece of his mind. He saw that she was standing on the pitch and was determined to order her off. As he got to within a few feet, she took off her small glasses, which had been perched on the end of her nose and glared at the approaching official. He stopped abruptly and the expression on his face changed instantly from fury to fear.

'Yes, young man, can I help you?' Miss Bell demanded in her finest, firm, headmistress' voice. It was a tone that Jimmy and the other young people of Barrowmarsh were all too familiar with

He gulped and started to stammer as she fixed him with a defiant glare.

'If ... if ... if you wouldn't mind, m ... m... madam ...' He gestured with his eyes towards the touchline.

'Speak up, man, don't mumble, there's a good chap.'

'Would ... would you mind, eh, leaving the pitch, if ... if ... if it's not too ... hum ... not too much trouble ... *please*?'

Miss Bell continued to glare at him. The crowd had fallen silent. All eyes, including those of the players, were on this confrontation.

Jimmy glanced at Grandad, who winked. 'This is like the cowboy film, *Gunfight at the OK Corral*!'

'P ... p ... please, m ... m ... madam?' The referee pleaded again.

Miss Bell replaced her spectacles, turned, sniffed, and threw back her head. She snorted, 'Uuh,' and marched back towards the fence.

A ripple of laughter spread through the crowd as the nervous official hurried back to the safety of the centre circle.

Yunara started to sing, 'Miss has got a red-card, Miss has got a red-card, na-na na na, na-na na na.'

Everyone laughed again.

The game was re-started and the twins were thrilled to see that nearly everyone in the crowd was clapping, cheering and chanting, '*Barrowmarsh, Barrowmarsh, Barrowmarsh.*' With only a minute or so of injury time left, they hoped the goal by Matthew Henderson would be enough to settle the result. The dream of reaching the FA Cup third-round for the first time ever was very close to becoming reality for the little village team.

'How long left?' Jimmy asked, hopping from one foot to the other.

'We're nearly there, bro; time must be up now.'

He glanced back at the pitch and saw that their dad had the ball on the edge of his own penalty area and in a dangerous position. 'LOOK OUT, DAD, CLEAR THE BALL.'

Two Llanpowys players charged forward.

Jenny repeated the warning. 'SEND IT UP-FIELD.'

'DON'T DITHER, YOUNG JONES,' Miss Bell screamed, 'BOOT IT INTO ORBIT!'

'I can't look,' Mr Braine gasped. 'We're going to throw it away, I just know it.'

Everything seemed to move in slow-motion and the

twins gripped each other's arms. Then, to their tremendous relief, Dad took one touch and clobbered the ball as hard as he could. It sailed up into the air and away into the other half of the field. The referee looked at his watch, put his whistle to his lips, and with a piercing blast brought about an almighty cheer from the relieved and delirious home supporters.

The players sportingly shook hands and the disappointed Llanpowys lads made their way towards Druid's Lodge to shower and change. The locals spilled onto the pitch to mob their heroes. Mr Braine and Miss Bell did a little jig-dance, round and round in a circle. They linked arms and sang, 'Wembley, Wembley, here we come, Wem-bley, here we come!'

'Brilliant,' Jenny and Jimmy ran onto the pitch, where all the Barrowmarsh players were waving to friends and family and raising their thumbs. 'They're acknowledging their historic achievement,' Jenny added, reading from her Treasure Book.

'Come on,' Jimmy called, and they danced around the pitch with everyone else, congratulating their players and clapping them off the field.

'Well done Mister Geraint,' Yunara said. 'Great saves.'

Bella Rogers threw her arms around her husband, Joe, the Thursdays' Number Nine, and their four children bobbed around them.

Jimmy and Jenny quickly found Dad and were delighted to see that Mum had already got to him, and that their grandparents were also on their way.

'We did it, Dad, we did it.' There was a clear mixture of joy and disbelief.

He grinned broadly, 'We sure did, and now we're into the third-round draw with the big-guns! Just think, we could be up against a Football League, Championship or even a Premier League club next. This is the dream, kids, the real deal ... we'll be on television ... Match of the Day and Sky Sport!'

'Our dad ... and our teacher ... on telly... Wow!'

Chapter Seven

The shorter days of December had set in, and at the start of another week in school everyone was talking about Saturday's match and the fantastic result against Llanpowys Casuals.

'It wasn't just the result,' Mr Frost beamed, 'it was the performance; every man giving his all for Barrowmarsh.'

The twins and their friends were making their way to morning assembly when Miss Bell came strutting down the corridor, smiling and whistling the tune of *Match of the Day*.

'Bore da, blant, and what a stupendous day it is.' The headmistress threw her arms out, dramatically. 'The sun is shining and Barrowmarsh Thursdays are in the draw for the third-round of the FA Cup, not any old cup, mind you, but the biggest, best and most important cup-competition in the whole wide world!' She looked up and saw the school caretaker shuffling towards her. 'Isn't that right, Mr Horton?'

Mr Horton seemed oblivious to everything around him and trundled past, muttering to himself. He toddled off down the corridor, mumbling and picking up a few pieces of paper that had blown in from the playground. Everyone in the school knew that Mr Horton talked to himself.

Jenny watched him go. 'There he goes again, in his soliloquy.'

Miss Bell put her hand over her mouth and laughed.

Jimmy knew what soliloquy meant because Jenny and Mr Frost had told him, but he was glad that it was not on his '*top hundred words*' sheet that his teacher had stuck in the back of his literacy book!

Mr Frost had heard the twins chatting about Mr Horton's habit, and commented, 'Hmm, he does appear to have a fondness for soliloquy, just like Hamlet in the Shakespeare play.'

Jenny scribbled the new word in her Treasure Book, then she and her brother chatted about *Hamlet*. They'd seen the film so they knew the main character talked to himself, just like Mr Horton.

Jenny really liked Jimmy's suggestion that Hamlet would be a good name for Mr Horton because of his soliloquy. His real name was Arnold but they decided that Hamlet Horton would sound much better so they told Mr Frost.

The teacher coughed and his mouth twitched. 'Now, now, you mustn't be disrespectful to our caretaker.' Then he turned and walked off down the corridor, chuckling and saying to himself, quietly, 'Hamlet Horton, I love it!'

The twins turned to each other and laughed as they realised Mr Frost was doing a soliloquy!

'Bore da, bawb.' Miss Bell greeted everyone in assembly. She read out a few messages then told everyone to sit up nicely to sing, 'Who Built the Ark?'

Mrs Morping played the introduction on the piano and everyone started singing ... 'Who built the Ark ...?'

Then Nails' voice boomed out, 'NO-ONE, NO-ONE.'

Jimmy and Jenny looked around and could see that everyone was doing the same.

'Who said that?' Mrs Morping had stopped playing and looked furious.

Nobody answered, and Jimmy noticed that Nails was sniggering.

Mrs Morping sat down and started playing again, calling out, 'From the beginning, children.'

'Who built the Ark?' everyone sang ...

'NO-ONE, NO-ONE,' Nails thundered, again.

'NO, NO, NO ...' Mrs Morping slammed her hand on the top of the piano, stood up and glared around the hall.

The twins looked at each other and put their hands to their mouths.

Miss Bell took off her glasses and Mr Frost's brow wrinkled as the enraged teacher walked around the piano and faced the pupils. Jenny could see Mrs Morping's feet planted wide, and her head jerking and darting looks in all directions.

'It's Noah, Noah, NO-AH, *not* NO-ONE.' Her face was red and blotchy, and her eyes bulged behind her glasses ... 'NOAH built the Ark!'

A ripple of giggles ran through the hall; all eyes were on Nails. Mrs Morping's searching gaze shot from one end of the hall to the other then settled on the spot where all other eyes were fixed. She lurched forward and stomped up the aisle. She stopped abruptly, folded her arms, and barked, 'Was it you, Norman?'

'No, Miss,' he answered, innocently and with exaggerated politeness, 'it wasn't me, Miss, it was Noah!'

A look of bewilderment spread across Mrs Morping's blotchy face. 'What *are* you talking about, Norman?'

'You asked if it was me, Miss … It wasn't, Miss … It wasn't me who built the Ark, Miss.' Nails' face was a picture of innocence. His eyes blinked rapidly. 'It was Noah, Miss … I didn't touch the Ark, honestly!'

The hall was in uproar with everyone holding their sides and laughing, and the twins could see Miss Bell covering her face with her hanky, pretending to cough.

Mrs Morping's face had changed from blotchy red to a dangerous shade of purple. She clenched her fists and stamped her feet. 'IT – IS – NOT – FUNNY!'

'But it *was* funny,' Jenny whispered to her brother and Yunara, who couldn't stop laughing!

Sam sat, expressionless. 'Noah built the Ark. It's in the Bible; the Book of Genesis, Chapter 6, from verse 9.'

Tears rolled down Yunara's face. She gasped for breath.

Mrs Morping pointed to the front of the hall; her finger was trembling. 'Norman Nailsworthy, you can go to Miss Bell at once! Go and explain yourself, do you hear me?'

But Miss Bell had dashed to the toilet with her hanky covering her face!

Mr Frost stood up. 'Now, everyone, listen in. Shall we all calm down and try to sing the rest of the song without any silly interruptions?' He looked directly at Nails and frowned. 'I'll have a word with you later, my boy!'

After the song, Miss Bell returned to the hall and talked about football before finishing assembly with a quiet moment of reflection. She asked everyone to think about the team's outstanding victory on the previous Saturday and what it meant to the village. She also suggested everyone might think about which club they'd like The Thursdays to meet in the third round!

After assembly the twins and their friends went back to their classroom where Mr Frost told them to get out their Maths books while he had a word with Nails. They pretended to be busy but everyone in the class was trying to listen to what their teacher was saying. He was speaking quietly, and Jenny opened up her Treasure Book, ran her finger down a page and whispered that he was being discreet and confidential.

Jimmy nodded. 'I'm sure you're right, sis.'

At the start of lunchtime the twins turned a corner to see Mum talking to Mrs Eastwood, who ran the 'Friends of Barrowmarsh Association'. Jenny held out her hand and stopped her brother. 'Shush, they're talking about Nails.' They stepped back into a doorway, out of sight.

'That Norman Nailsworthy can be a very naughty boy at times.' Mrs Eastwood spoke in a loud whisper. 'He's really beyond; we've never had anyone quite like him at the school before ...'

Mrs Eastwood looked over one shoulder then the other. 'But then, what can you expect with a mother like his? She's never been along to one of our parent-meetings. I don't know what she has to hide ... Social Services are involved, I've heard ... not one of *our* sort, I'm sure!'

From the doorway, the twins noticed that Mum kept saying 'mmm' and that her eyes were almost closed as if she were half asleep. She nodded her head and did a strange sort of smile every now and then.

Mrs Eastwood leaned in and whispered, 'I've heard he was ... excluded from his last school!'

Mum looked at her watch. 'Well, it's been lovely talking to you, but I really have to dash!' Mrs Eastwood walked away, and Mum stomped into her office, muttering, 'That woman is such a snob ... she is insufferable!'

Jenny's eyes widened. 'Time to go, bro.' Jimmy agreed.

Mum's mood hadn't improved by the evening. She stormed into the kitchen with a piece of crumpled paper in her hand.

'Uh-oh,' Jimmy thought.

'And what is this, my lad?' Her lips were tight and her eyes glaring.

'Oops!' Jimmy said. 'I forgot about that.'

'I can see that. I found it in the bottom of your bag.' She slammed the piece of paper onto the table. It was a note from Mr Frost inviting Mum and Dad into school to see his work. He'd hidden the note in the bottom of his bag knowing full well that his books weren't the tidiest in the class. Jenny had handed over her note as soon as they'd arrived home from school.

Jimmy knew he'd been rumbled. He narrowed his eyes, wrinkled his nose, put his teeth together ... and gave Jenny *a look*.

He guessed he was about to land in a whole heap of trouble when Mum frowned, tapped her foot and folded her arms menacingly. His fears were confirmed when she said, 'I know very well that you had a note, my lad, I typed and prepared it myself so that Mr Frost could put the time of the appointment on. You seem to forget that I actually work at the school!'

Jimmy looked on helplessly as Mum emptied his school bag, which she described as disgusting. 'Clean this mess out now,' she growled. There was an almighty row. Teabag hid under a chair. Jimmy was sent to his room with, 'You haven't heard the last of this, my boy,' following him up the stairs like a snarling dog snapping at his heels. Jimmy reflected that whenever his mum called him 'my boy' he really wished he wasn't her boy!

He wasn't allowed to watch *Mudlarking Magic* on TV. He realised that trying to hide the note had been a massive mistake, but he'd done it because he knew exactly what would happen: Mum and Dad would go to the school, look at Jenny's work and smile a lot. They'd read her stories and would certainly comment on her neat handwriting. Then they would talk to Mr Frost who'd smile and say things like, 'Good of you to come, Jack; nice to see you, Jayne, please take a seat ... Now, about Jenny ...' Then he would say lots of things that teachers say, like, 'problem-solving is excellent ... blah, blah, blah ... key skills ... blah, blah, blah ... very attentive and hard-working ... blah, blah, blah.' He would smile, of course, and say, 'Jayne, Jack, your daughter is a credit to you!'

Then, Mr Frost would speak quietly, lean in closer and say something like ... 'He's very bright ... good skills ... lots of potential, but ... football! He can sometimes rush his work because all he seems to think about is football.'

Jimmy imagined Mum glaring at Dad and saying something like, 'Does that remind you of anyone, Jack?'

As Jimmy sat in his room he thought about Nails. He knew that getting excluded from school was very serious and that parents also received an official letter from the school's Governors, which, he guessed, would result in an awful lot of unhappiness and upset for the whole family. He decided that not even Nails deserved that.

Jimmy knew that his own behaviour hadn't been bad enough for him to be excluded from school but he also knew that he *had* done wrong, and that he was lucky to get off with just being grounded for a few hours.

During his time in 'solitary confinement', as Grandad called it, he pondered what he could do without his computer or television. After a bit of thought he hit upon the idea of finding a new word from a dictionary and learning its meaning. Jenny always used her Treasure Book to impress and Sam could remember the most complicated things without even writing them down. So, he decided to try and find a really long word so that he could show off to his sister and friends. It wasn't long before he struck gold ... he pulled a dictionary from a shelf and turned to somewhere near the middle ... p ... pa ... pi ... po ... pr ... pro ... Then he found the word that he knew would do nicely ... *procrastinate*. He wrote it on a piece of paper and quickly added the meaning, 'to postpone or to put off'. He practiced using it and was determined to look for a chance to impress.

He didn't have to wait long. After a couple of hours he was allowed out of his room, and after having a *pep talk*, and apologising, he went to the kitchen where he found Mum grumbling and holding a basket of laundry.

'I suppose I should get on with this ironing.' She put the basket down, sighed and then muttered, 'I hate ironing.'

Jimmy seized the opportunity. 'Oh, for goodness sake, Mum, stop procrastinating.'

She turned sharply and looked at him. 'What did you just say?'

'It's not swearing,' he said, quickly and defiantly.

'I know it's not a swear-word, Jimmy, I'm simply impressed with your vocabulary; maybe I should ground you more often! So, would you like to do the ironing for me?'

He stepped back and spluttered, 'No, thank you, I'm sure you are far better at it than I am.'

Mum chuckled ...

Jimmy shook his head and muttered, 'Grown-ups can be really strange creatures!'

Chapter Eight

By play-time on Tuesday morning everyone's attention had switched from the fantastic win over Llanpowys to the next round of The Cup. The whole school babbled and chatted excitedly about the FA Cup draw, which was due to take place just before lunchtime. Everyone was in a bubbly mood; everyone apart from Nails, that is. He skulked along close to the wall at the far end of the playground, his hood over his head and his feet dragging along the floor. He was a solitary and miserable figure, scowling at no-one in particular, and viciously kicking stones as he plodded around. Every so often he would push at a younger child. Most people, however, avoided the bad-tempered and bad-mannered boy.

The repetitive ding-a-ling of the school bell was soon joined by the scuffling thuds of feet on tarmac as jostling youngsters made their way to their class lines in front of the main entrance. Miss Roberts, the teacher on playground duty, stopped ringing the bell and walked briskly to the front of the assembled school. Without a word she jogged on the spot, raising her arms above her head as she did so. Everyone copied. After a few moments the teacher changed to a two-footed skipping action and again all the pupils followed; all except Nails, of course, who stood as still as a goal-post, muttering and mumbling to himself.

After a few more vigorous exercises, the young, track-suited teacher stopped and smiled. 'That's the way, guys, now we're alert and energised and ready for the rest of the morning's learning; fighting fit and prepared for anything.'

Miss Roberts nodded to her left. 'Ffion, you can lead your class; David, you can take yours, and Amanda can take Miss Morping's class. Sam, I'm putting you in charge of Mr Frost's class, and I know I can trust you to lead the rest of the school inside.'

Sam stood to attention and marched off with purpose. One by one the classes followed, weaving and winding their way up the ramp, through the opened doors and into the school's entrance hall. Everyone smiled at 'Miss' as they passed. Nails scowled.

Back in class the topic of conversation was, once again, football:

'Hope we get a home draw ...'

'It would be better to play away in a big stadium ...'

'Who do you think we'll get, Newcastle, Bristol City ... The Swans?'

Nails pulled his sweatshirt up over his head but the rest of the class erupted into a babble of questions and opinions as everyone wanted to speak at once.

Mr Frost stood in the middle of the room. 'Excuse me, class, but could we please have a bit of order so that we can get on with the morning's lessons ... I understand how you feel; you are excited. *I'm* excited, I mean ... the FA Cup third-round ... wow!'

Mr Frost stood, motionless, staring at the window with a silly smile on his face. The class, too, became still, as silence settled like gently falling leaves and twenty eight hushed faces looked up expectantly at their grinning, far-away teacher ...

Jimmy nudged Jenny. 'Do you think he's fallen asleep?'

'No,' she whispered, 'he's enjoying his reverie.'

'Enjoying his what?' Yunara asked.

'His reverie ... his daydream,' she explained. 'He's probably imagining himself walking up those steps at Wembley to collect The Cup.'

'Hey,' Jimmy said, quietly, 'what things are taken to Wembley every year but are never used?'

Jenny looked puzzled. 'I don't know. What things *are* taken to Wembley every year but never used?'

'The Cup ribbons in the losing team's colours, of course,' he laughed, as Jenny and Yunara smiled.

Mr Frost stirred suddenly. 'Ahem ... now where was I? Oh yes, lessons.'

Everyone laughed and Mr Frost grinned, sheepishly.

Soon, all the classrooms of Barrowmarsh Primary were into the swing of morning activities. Mr Frost's class was busy with a Maths data-handling topic. Some groups were recording the previous Saturday's Premiership and Championship football results. Others were tallying points, working out goal differences and entering all sorts of information into data bases ...

Jimmy whistled as he tapped away at a keyboard. 'How can Mr Frost call this sort of stuff work?'

Yunara grinned broadly. 'It's work and it's fun at the same time.'

Jimmy's group was looking at the football results in

newspapers and putting crowd-attendance information into their iPads. Another group was devising a Maths game, based on an FA Cup competition, using dice and counters.

Jenny and Sam's friends were using the Internet to find and record information on leading goal-scorers from all Premiership and Championship clubs. Sam was able to remember every detail with just one glance, and was able to give all the statistics to his friends without looking back to the screen.

Nails was supposed to be part of Jimmy's group but, apart from muttering about how much he hated football, he kept getting up and walking around the class. Mr Frost offered to work with him on a dinosaur data-base.

Suddenly there was an almighty shriek that caused several people to leap from their chairs like startled grasshoppers.

Sarah Rogers was yelling, '*Mr Frost, Mr Frost ... come quickly!*'

The teacher, who was trying to make a few suggestions to Nails, looked up in alarm. 'Whatever's the matter, Sarah?'

'It's Henry the Eighth, Mr Frost,' Sarah wailed, 'he's not in his cage; I think he's escaped!' (Henry was the class hamster, and the eighth hamster that Mr Frost had owned. They'd all been called Henry.)

There was pandemonium in the classroom, a tumble of bodies, as everyone dropped to their hands and knees and set off crawling between chairs and tables looking for their cheeky, chubby little hamster.

'Now everyone,' Mr Frost called out over the din, 'stay

calm and, for goodness sake, stay still. I'll just make sure, but if he has escaped we don't want to frighten him and we certainly don't want anyone to stand on him.'

Jenny screamed frantically at the thought of someone accidentally treading on him. 'Oh no, Henry, Henry, where are you, Henry?'

Mr Frost walked carefully over to Henry's cage, and was surprised to find its door wide open. He put his hand inside and searched amongst the toys, the balls of bedding, the exercise wheel and Henry's little house. Nothing! He looked at the cage and pondered. 'How on earth did that door open? It's usually very secure.'

Everyone looked anxious, except for Nails, who leaned back on his chair with a big grin on his face. 'Looks like he's done a runner, *Sir*. Can't say I blame him.'

Mr Frost's eyes narrowed but when he spoke his voice was quiet and calm. 'Do you know anything about this, Norman?'

'Not a thing, *Sir*.' Nails smirked. 'He must have got fed up of all this talk about football and decided to go for a little stroll.' He laughed at his own joke.

'Mr Frost, Mr Frost, I can see him!' It was Sarah again, squealing and flapping her arms. 'Quick, he's under that computer table, behind those wires!'

'Well done, Sarah. Now, stay calm, everyone.' Mr Frost held his hand up. 'Stay perfectly still and leave this to me ... it's important we don't startle him.' He got down onto his hands and knees and crept, stealthily, towards the computer table.

'Quickly, Sir,' Jenny pleaded, 'before Benny gets to him.'

Mr Frost stopped in his tracks. 'Oh Lord, I'd forgotten about Benny.'

Benny, the school cat, was a huge, grumpy, grey tabby who usually spent his day sleeping on his favourite shelf above a radiator in the school hall. If he wasn't sleeping, however, it meant that he was hungry and off in search of food.

Mr Frost started moving again, quickening his pace as he crawled towards the computer table. 'Don't panic, folks, we'll soon have this under control. Just … just stay calm.'

'Want any help, *Sir*?' Nails drawled.

'Not at the moment, Norman, thank you, but I'm sure we'll have a little chat about this later.'

'I'm glad Teabag's not here,' Jenny whispered.

Jimmy agreed, thinking about the chaos their scruffy little apricot poodle would have caused.

Mr Frost had moved so that his head was under the table.

'Nice Henry, come to me, nice hamster. Lovely Henry, come to Mr Frosty Wosty.'

Nails sniggered.

Everyone held their breath as their teacher inched forward towards the small, golden ball of fur. Henry sat on his haunches, his tiny hands rubbing his whiskers, unconcerned as Mr Frost's hands moved slowly towards their goal. Suddenly, he lunged forward but only succeeded in grabbing a handful of computer cables. The wary hamster darted across the aisle and scuttled under the Maths-Games table …

'Drat!' Mr Frost's face was red, and still on hands and

knees he scrambled across the aisle. Jenny thought he looked so silly and the others laughed too.

'It's just as well you don't play in goal for The Thursdays, Sir,' Jenny said, and everyone laughed again as the harassed and puffing teacher looked up at them.

'Very funny, Jennifer ... now, everyone, try to be still and quiet, please. Sam, Yunara, Sarah ... watch the other side of this table; make sure he doesn't escape.'

Once again Mr Frost dived in and, sure enough, Henry shot in the opposite direction. This time, however, Sam was one step ahead. He held a large plastic container, usually used for coloured counters, directly in the path of the escaping hamster.

'Got him,' Yunara yelled, triumphantly. 'Well done Sam.'

Mr Frost pulled out a hankie and wiped his face. 'Yes, good thinking, Sam, you're a genius.'

The class cheered loudly and Sam beamed with pleasure as he walked to the hamster cage and placed Henry safely back inside. The little ball of fur trundled over to his food bowl, picked up a sunflower seed and nibbled away contentedly, obviously none the worse for his little adventure.

Mr Frost heaved himself up from the floor and flopped into a chair, panting for breath. 'I'm not as fit as I used to be.'

'That's the trouble with all of you in that second-rate excuse for a football team,' Nails muttered under his breath but loud enough for everyone to hear. 'You're not fit enough or good enough.'

Everyone watched in silence as Mr Frost stroked his

chin calmly. Jimmy knew that he would have been angry and upset if someone had said something like that to him, but he was full of admiration as their teacher just looked at Nails, smiled gently and said, 'Well done, everyone; now that the little rascal is safely back in his cage we can all get on with our Maths.'

Mr Frost strolled around the class to see how everyone was getting on and Jimmy knew he had to ask him a question.

'Why didn't you get angry, Sir, when Nails said those nasty things about you not being fit?'

Mr Frost puffed out his cheeks and sat down. 'I'm a teacher, Jimmy; I'm a professional. It wouldn't do for me to lose my temper now would it? I prefer to show others the right way to do things.'

'But don't you ever get upset, Sir?'

'Sometimes, Jimmy, of course I get upset, but I have to stay in control, even when I'm angry. It is my job to show you and the others a responsible way to act.'

Sam looked up. 'My dad says we should always think carefully about the consequences before we act.'

Yunara agreed. 'Yes, when we were in Africa my father ...'

'*Why don't you all just shut up!*' Nails kicked at a chair, which clattered to the floor.

Mr Frost turned sharply. 'That's quite enough of that, Norman! What is your problem?'

Sam quickly put his hand up. 'Nails is unhappy because he doesn't have a father.'

Nails pulled his sweatshirt up over his head again and everyone else sat in a stunned silence.

The white-faced teacher turned to Sam. 'Thank you, Sam, you're very perceptive.'

For once, Jenny didn't touch her Treasure Book.

Mr Frost walked over to Nails, picked up the fallen chair and sat down. 'We can talk about this anytime you want, Norman ... you're amongst friends ... give us a chance, trust us.'

Just then, the classroom door swung open and Miss Bell swept into the room carrying a portable radio. 'Good morning, Mr Frost; bore da, class,' and before waiting for a reply she announced the purpose of her visit. She plugged in the radio and switched it on. 'I was thinking that it was high time this school did some media studies,'

Mr Frost stood, open-mouthed, as Miss Bell took over. 'Now pay attention, children, I thought we would start with broadcasts of a topical nature.' With that, she looked at her watch and turned up the volume on the radio.

'This is the BBC Sports-desk ... and now we can go over, live, to Lancaster Gate for the third round draw of the Football Association Challenge Cup.'

Jimmy looked at Yunara and they smiled.

'Good old Miss Bell,' Jenny whispered.

The headmistress looked over her little reading glasses. 'Less of the *old* if you don't mind, Jennifer, my dear. Now shush, everyone, let's listen to the draw.'

Mr Frost grinned and sat on the edge of a table. The class sat quietly and listened very carefully. Jimmy could hear the rustling of the bag that contained the numbered balls. He'd seen them on television and remembered they looked like snooker balls, and that each one had a number representing a team.

97

'A few numbers to listen out for,' the announcer said, 'Arsenal are number one, Chelsea number fourteen, Manchester City are number forty one and the minnows from Barrowmarsh are number ten.'

Murmurs rolled around the classroom. He said a few other numbers but they could now only think about the all-important number ten. Mister Frost nodded to Miss Bell who seemed impatient and anxious for the Football Association officials to get on with things. Everyone could hear the clickety-clack of the balls knocking against each other as one of the officials shook them around in the bag to mix them up.

'This is so exciting,' Jenny whispered from her table and her brother agreed, finding it difficult to keep still. Yunara was grinning and Sam was frowning and putting all his badges in a line in front of him. Megan had moved to sit beside Nails and was gently persuading him to pull his sweatshirt from his head.

As they listened the numbered balls were drawn from the bag. The teams who were to play each other were announced in a hushed voice, almost like that of a snooker commentator. 'Number sixty two ... Rotherham ... will play number twenty six ... Everton ... Number forty five ... Middlesbrough ... will play ... number sixty seven ... Torquay United ...'

Sam had worked out that the teams were in alphabetical order and that their numbers corresponded accordingly.

'Of course,' Yunara nodded, 'that's why Arsenal are number one.'

The draw seemed to go on forever. They heard that

Chelsea were to play Bolton Wanderers, and that Swansea City would be up against Bradford City. Cardiff had a home tie against West Ham, Arsenal were drawn against Wigan, and there were to be two local derbies between Hereford United and Shrewsbury Town, and Newport County against Wrexham.

The tension was becoming unbearable; Mr Frost was twisting a piece of paper around his finger and Miss Bell paced up and down the room ...

But then ...

'Number ten ... Barrowmarsh Thursdays,' the announcer's voice declared ... 'will play ...'

Jimmy looked around and could see that everyone in the room appeared frozen as the announcer said, 'Number forty-two ...'

He then said the name of the team. Jimmy blinked rapidly and watched as Miss Bell suddenly stopped pacing, as if someone had pressed pause on a remote control. Her mouth was wide open in disbelief. Mister Frost went very pale and dropped the piece of gnarled paper he'd been twisting.

Jenny looked at Jimmy and stammered, 'D ... d ... did he just say ... *United*?'

'Yes, I think so.'

'What? Do you mean *THE United*?'

Jimmy simply nodded, trying to take in what he'd just heard ... Their very own little village team, the team that Mr Frost was captain of, the team that their dad was manager of, would be playing at home to one of the world's top clubs; Premier League and European champions ... the great United!

The remainder of the draw went unheard as a wave of excitement washed over the classroom and turned into a din of whoops, screeches and babbling chatter. Miss Bell said something to Mr Frost, then rushed from the room.

The teacher held up his hands. 'Okay guys ... Please guys,' he said again, 'let's have some order so that we can ... discuss what we've just heard.'

'Does this mean we'll be doing *probability* in Maths, Sir?' Jenny asked. 'What are the chances of our little team beating the great United and reaching the next round of the cup?'

'Absolutely no chance at all, I'd say,' Nails muttered, miserably, pulling his hood up. 'If I were you, I wouldn't even bother turning up for the game.'

Everyone, Mr Frost and Megan included, sat and looked on in silence.

Mr Frost got up from the table and walked slowly across to the window. He stood with his back to the class and with his hands in his pockets. Jimmy was wondering how he'd react this time after all that had gone on with Nails that morning.

Their teacher was calm and quiet. 'Do you know what, class? We probably *will* be beaten by the magnificent European champions ... but we have earned the right to be on the same field as those famous players. We don't play for money – we play for fun. We have jobs away from football yet we will play against United and we will give our best effort. We won't worry about the result, we will be proud to have taken part for our village ... for our wonderful, little Barrowmarsh.'

For a second or two the room was completely silent, then Megan stood and started clapping; one by one they all stood and joined in the applause.

Mr Frost walked across to Nails, smiled and said, quietly, 'One day, Norman, you will do something you're extremely proud of ... I'm sure of it, my lad, I'm sure of it.'

Chapter Nine

At the end of school on that never-to-be-forgotten December day, the day of the FA Cup third-round draw, everyone made their way across the playground chattering excitedly about the prospects of playing the mighty United at their very own Parc Y Derwydd. Things were about to become even more exciting. 'Look!' gasped Jenny, holding out her hands. 'It's snowing!'

The grass of the village green was already stiff and crisp with frost and there had been a layer of ice covering the surface of the pond for several days. Yunara and Jandir danced about, catching snowflakes in their laughing mouths. Yunara's eyes were bright and wide as she shouted with glee and told the twins that they'd never seen real snow before. Their foster parents, Harry and Kalisha, laughed heartily as they tried to get them to put gloves and scarves on to keep warm for their walk home.

Megan strolled past. 'Bye, munchkins, see you tomorrow.'

'Unless we get snowed in and can't get to school,' Jenny said, hopefully.

Megan chuckled. 'Nice try, Jenny, you only live the other side of The Green.' She waved and walked off up High Street.

The village looked so wonderfully wintery in the deepening darkness of late afternoon. The windows of the shops in the High Street and the houses around The

Green were glowing warmly with cosy, twinkling lights and Christmas trees. Most of the front doors welcomed visitors with holly wreaths, mistletoe and vivid splashes of green and red.

The snow was settling and Jimmy was able to make footprints. 'It's not deep enough for snowballs yet, but maybe in the morning it will be really, really deep and we can build a snowman and put a Thursdays football shirt on him.'

Jenny was delighted. 'And we can make a big snow-ball for him to play with.'

The twins laughed, but Sam frowned. 'I don't think a snowman will be able to kick a snow-ball.'

'Right enough, Sam,' Jenny answered, cheerfully, 'but it will look good.'

Jimmy and Jenny's mum had arranged with Sam's parents for him to have tea with them at Druid's Lodge.

Across the village green they could see their home. Lots of coloured lights shone round the windows and there were lovely, sparkly fairy lights in the trees and bushes at the front of the guest-house. Outside the front door there was a huge and cheerful Christmas tree that the twins had helped decorate. As they walked across the darkening white of the village green, Jenny pointed to the colourful reflections on the ice-covered surface of the village pond.

They were having lots of fun and they took their time crossing The Green. They scrunched and crunched the frosty grass and bounced around in the thickening, fluffy snow that was now falling rapidly and settling on the frozen ground.

'Look who's behind us,' Jenny hissed, suddenly.

They turned to see Nails trudging along slowly, his hood up, hands deep in his pockets and his feet kicking out angrily at the swirling snow. Sam pulled up his hood and moved closer to Jenny.

'Don't worry, Sam, he doesn't seem to be bothered with us; he's walking home alone, as usual.' Jimmy thought about Nails and wished that he'd been able to offer him a kind word. He knew that Nails never had a friend to walk with, and wondered if there was anything they could do to help.

As they approached Druid's Lodge an apricot flash darted from the side door and Teabag lolloped through the snow towards them. He always ran to greet them when they returned from school but, with the falling snow, he seemed even more excited than usual.

'Teabag,' they shouted, together, 'come on boy ... who's a lovely doggy?'

He bounded forward, tail wagging, yapping and snapping at the flurrying snow. Suddenly, he spotted a raven skittering across the frozen pond and he changed direction, barking wildly as he galloped towards the bird and the pond.

Jimmy was frantic. '*No, Teabag, no!*'

'*Stop, Teabag, come back,*' Jenny screamed ...

It seemed like a horrible dream as they watched their little dog hit the ice covered pond. The raven flew off quickly and Teabag's legs slithered and scampered in a desperate attempt to steady himself.

The twins ran towards the pond, followed by Sam, but they could only watch, helplessly, as the little dog toppled and spun across the frozen surface. As they reached the pond's edge they heard a squeaking crack, followed by a splash and a loud yelp.

'TEABAG!'

They peered through the gloom of dusk. The lights of Druid's Lodge threw some illumination across the pond but they couldn't see Teabag. He'd disappeared!

The three stood, immobile and staring; their minds and bodies numb. The momentary silence shattered as a loud splashing noise wrenched them back to reality. They inched forward to the very edge of the sheet of ice. Their eyes strained, searching for something in the vicinity of the sound but all they could see was the dark, sharp and ugly shape near the pond's centre where the ice had broken.

They started yelling again, frantically calling Teabag's name, then paused, listening and hoping for some response. There was a moment's silence then a loud whoosh and a lot more splashing.

'*There*,' Jenny screamed. Sam and Jimmy looked to where her finger was pointing, and spotted Teabag's bedraggled head bobbing up and down. His eyes were huge. He was clearly terrified and they could see that he was desperately scrabbling at the ice with his front paws, trying to find a grip; trying to pull himself up out of the freezing water.

They watched in horror as the little dog slid below the surface.

'*Teabag, Teabag, come back, come back ... jump out ... please ...*'

The dog's head popped up again but he seemed to be

losing his strength and his fight to pull himself from the paralysing water.

'Oh no,' Sam mumbled. 'The octopus will get him.'

Jenny started to wail.

Suddenly, the twins were pushed to one side as someone barged between them and scrambled onto the pond's frozen covering. They looked on in disbelief as Nails spread himself wide and started out, crawling slowly across the ice to where Teabag's head bobbed up and down. As he eased forward, making slow but steady progress, the others could hear the creaking of the ice as it groaned and grumbled under Nails' hefty bulk. Jimmy could hear him talking soothingly to Teabag as he crawled. 'Hold on, there's a good boy ... Hold on, I'm coming to get you.'

As Nails got to within a few feet of the jagged hole, Sam and the twins heard a sickening crack and knew that the ice was starting to break up. Nails stretched his hand towards a now frantic Teabag but he was still a few inches short. He stretched again and another loud crack tore through the gloom. They could see that the creaking, squeaking ice was disintegrating at an alarming rate.

'Just a bit more,' Nails was saying, 'I'm almost there ... can't ... quite ... make it.'

'I know what we can do.' Sam had a sudden thought, and without waiting for a response he ran over to a near-by tree. Within seconds he was back, dragging a long, slim branch that had fallen from the old Horse-Chestnut.

Nails looked over his shoulder. 'That's it Sam; perfect,

just what I need ... just slide the branch over to me. Don't step onto the ice, though, it won't take our combined weight.'

Sam knelt at the pond's edge. He took careful aim, and very slowly pushed the tree-branch across what remained of the icy surface. Nails twisted to his side in an effort to grab the branch. The ice rumbled and groaned again and a terrifying crack rang out as the surface split and a gaping rift opened up.

'We need help,' Sam said, calmly. 'Nails can't swim properly.'

Nails looked over his shoulder. 'I don't need to be reminded of that right now, Sammy boy.'

Jenny realised that Sam was right and that they had little time to waste. She turned and sprinted off towards Druid's Lodge.

Nails, meanwhile, had grabbed the branch and had thrust it forward across the ice. It now straddled the hole in which Teabag bobbed about, whining and whimpering pitifully. The little dog seemed to understand what Nails intended; he thrust himself upwards and on the second attempt clamped his jaws around the tree branch.

'Good boy, Teabag,' Jimmy yelled. 'Hold on, we'll soon get you out.'

It had become very dark and much colder, and the snow was falling thicker than ever.

Nails edged forward and yet another hideous crack tore through the snowy, early-evening air. 'Just another inch or two,' he gasped out, painfully. 'I'm nearly there ...'

Jimmy yelled his encouragement. 'Just try to hold on,

Nails, Jenny's gone for help; someone will be here very soon.'

Jimmy and Sam looked up at the sound of thumping and thudding feet; Dad, Mum, Mr Frost and Martin, the policeman, were hurtling across the village green ...

Suddenly, Nails lunged forward and grabbed Teabag's collar, but the violent movement was too much for the fragile ice, which shattered and fragmented, plunging Nails into the dark and freezing water.

Everyone gasped and stared, their mouths open in shock as the large boy disappeared beneath the icy surface.

'He can't swim,' Mr Frost cried out.

Before anyone could react there was a tremendous splash and Nails' soaking head, shoulders and upper body shot up, like a cork, out of the water. The onlookers could see that he had a struggling Teabag gripped firmly under one arm, while his free hand stretched frantically for the now floating wooden branch.

PC Martin jumped through the bobbing shards of ice, and took two dragging paces forward. '*Don't follow*,' he shouted over his shoulder, 'it gets much deeper.' He pushed on, his shoulders dropping below the pond's surface. 'Hold on Norman, I'll be with you in a second.'

Nails' eyes were wide and his mouth open; he was too shocked to respond. Despite his grip on the wooden branch his face kept slipping into the water, but he still managed to hold Teabag's head above the surface.

PC Martin was getting closer but was having difficulty swimming because of the chunks of broken ice. 'The branch, Norman, the branch, try to push it towards me, I'm almost there.'

At last, Nails moved. He shoved the branch towards the advancing policeman. Mr Frost flung off his shoes and leapt into the water. He waded then swam forward, grabbing the belt of PC Martin's trousers. Dad jumped in and quickly grabbed Mr Frost and then, in an instant, Mum was in the water, holding Dad. They'd formed a human chain! Mum looked back sternly at the twins and snapped, 'Don't even think about it!'

PC Martin stretched forward, his fingers flailing but he couldn't quite reach the branch. From where they stood on the embankment, the twins could hear Nails' teeth chattering and they could see, even in the darkness and through the falling snow, that his face was very, very pale.

'*Let go of the dog*,' PC Martin shouted, but Nails shook his head and continued to cling tightly to Teabag.

Sirens screamed and Jenny, Sam and Jimmy reeled around to see the dazzling, blue, flashing lights of a fire engine, an ambulance and a police car as they sped past Druid's Lodge. They drove over the pavement and crossed the snow covered grass before stopping next to the youngsters at the edge of the pond.

At that very moment, PC Martin lunged again, grabbed the wooden branch and started hauling Nails and Teabag towards him. 'Good lad,' he encouraged, 'hold on tight, you're nearly there.'

The fire-fighters were in the water and pulling at the human chain. Mum pulled Dad; he pulled Mr Frost, and Mr Frost pulled PC Martin who, by this time had a firm hold on Nails ... Nails still gripped Teabag, who was licking Nails' face.

Two more ambulances arrived as the fire-fighters

hauled everyone from the water and onto the snow covered bank. Paramedics quickly wrapped foil blankets around PC Martin, Nails and, of course, Teabag. They were taken into the waiting ambulances along with Mum, Dad, and Mr Frost.

Many villagers had arrived on the scene by this time, alerted by the commotion and the noise of the emergency vehicles.

'Don't worry, Jayne,' Grandad called. 'We'll take care of the young 'uns ... and the guest-house. Just get yourselves checked over to make sure you're okay.'

Dad muttered and mumbled as he was led into the back of the ambulance. 'Nothing wrong with me ... just a bit wet and cold, that's all ... nothing a good hot toddy wouldn't put right.'

'*Jack*!' Mum scolded, 'Behave yourself and do as you're told.'

'Yes, my love, but we'll have to make sure a vet has a good look at Teabag.'

Mum chuckled. 'You and that pooch!'

Jenny and Jimmy looked to their Grandma, who assured them that everyone would be fine; they just needed to be checked over at the hospital. She had been a nurse as a young woman, and she explained the need to eliminate the dangers of shock and hypothermia, and to make sure they'd not picked up any toxic bacterial-infections.

'*What*?' Jenny shrieked.

Grandma held up her hand, reassuringly. 'Don't be alarmed, they're in safe hands and will be as right as rain by tomorrow, so don't worry, my dear.'

'It's not that,' Jenny spluttered. 'Where's my schoolbag? I need my Treasure Book ... what was that phrase, toxic bactewhatsits?'

Mum and Dad arrived home from the hospital later that night, and they also had Teabag with them. They told Jimmy and Jenny exactly what Grandma had already said, that everyone was going to be okay. Mr Frost had also been allowed to return home, but PC Martin and Nails were being kept in overnight, just as a precaution.

The twins ran to Teabag and hugged him a lot. He did his smiley face and wagged his tail wildly. Dad took the excited dog from them, tucked him into a blanket, placed him in his basket and brought him a ham roll from the kitchen. The twins suddenly remembered to hug Mum and Dad, too!

The next day in a very snowy and wintery Barrowmarsh School everyone was chattering about the dramatic events of the evening before and, of course, everyone wanted to know about Teabag.

Mr Frost assured the class that no one had suffered any long-term ill effects.

Sam tugged at Mr Frost's jacket. 'Mr Frost?'

'Yes, Sam, what is it?'

'Did you see the octopus in the water?'

'No Sam, there's no octopus in the pond. That was only a silly story that was meant to tease you.'

Sam looked across the table. 'But Jimmy told me ...'

'It really was *just* a story, Sam.' Mr Frost smiled, then added, 'I forgot to say, Sam, well done for your incredibly quick thinking. That tree-branch helped in a number of ways; things could have been a lot worse if you hadn't acted so promptly ... Thank you, Sam.'

Sam shrugged. 'Could I have a 'well-done' badge, please, Mr Frost?'

'Of course, Sam. You definitely deserve a badge for your sharp thinking.' He sat on the edge of a table and looked around the room at everyone. 'I think the person who deserves the most praise for his gallant actions, however, is Norman Nailsworthy. He'll be coming out of hospital later today and I should think he'll be off school for a couple of days. Miss Bell is popping in to see him later on this morning.'

'Perhaps we could make a nice, big 'Get Well Soon' card for him,' Jenny suggested.

'Yes, and we could get Teabag to put a paw-print on it,' Yunara added.

Megan grinned and took a few large pieces of coloured card from a storage tray.

Jenny pulled her purse from her school bag. 'And we could buy Nails some scrumptious sweets and a few comics from our pocket money.'

Mr Frost rubbed his hands together and beamed. 'Perfect, everyone, let's show Norman what we think of his bravery, and what we think of *him*.'

'Good old Nails,' they all agreed.

Chapter Ten

The fun and excitement of the Christmas and winter celebrations came and went in Barrowmarsh. The snow had thawed and everyone recovered from the ordeal of the frozen pond.

A few days after his heroic deeds on Druid's Pond, Nails was visited by the twins, with Yunara and Sam. They knew very little about Nails or his family, so they were quite nervous about what to expect. Miss Bell had called several times and reported on his progress to the whole school during assembly. She'd also said that she and Nails' mum had got on like a house on fire.

The friends were greeted by Mrs Nailsworthy and Nails, who welcomed them with a huge cake, especially made for the occasion.

Sam eagerly accepted a large slice of the chocolate-covered cake, which he said was his favourite. 'Thank you, Mrs Nailsworthy. Why do you use that stick with a small ball on the end when you walk?'

Jenny nudged him. '*Sam!*'

'That's all right Jenny, I don't mind Sam asking.'

Nails poured orange juice for all his visitors and then poured a cup of tea for his mum and placed it in her hand.

'Thank you, cariad; now make sure you get a drink and some cake for yourself.'

Yunara and the twins exchanged glances. They would never have imagined the fearsome Nails doing such things.

'This cake is the best I've ever tasted, Mrs Nailsworthy. Did you make it yourself?' Yunara took another big bite.

Nails' mum leaned in closer and screwed up her eyes. 'It's Yunara, isn't it? What a beautiful name.'

'Thank you, Mrs Nailsworthy. My brother's called Jandir, and we're from Africa.'

'How delightful; Norman's told me all about you ... about all of you, in fact. But I believe you asked me a question, Sam.' She looked around the room carefully, as if looking for Sam. 'The thing is, Sam, I can't see very well. In fact, I don't have much vision at all, but Norman is a tremendous help to me.'

The youngsters looked at each other. Yunara's eyes widened and Jenny put a hand to her cheek. Then they stared at Nails, open-mouthed.

Sam was unfazed. 'Were you born with your condition, Mrs Nailsworthy? I was born with mine.'

Jenny covered her face with her hands and cringed at Sam's directness. She cleared her throat noisily and attempted to change the subject. Nails scratched his nose and lowered his eyes, but said nothing.

Mrs Nailsworthy smiled. 'No, I wasn't born with it, Sam, and thank you for asking. Many people avoid mentioning my blindness. It was the result of a car accident about five years ago.'

Sam nodded. 'Is that what happened to Nails' dad? Could I have some more cake, please?'

Jenny sat frozen in her seat, her eyes shut tight, and her hands gripping the edges of the chair.

Mrs Nailsworthy smiled. 'More cake for everyone

please, cariad, and perhaps you could tell your friends all about it.' She turned her head towards Yunara, Sam and the twins. 'We've talked about this and, after everything that has happened, Norman feels he owes you an explanation.'

Nails pulled out a kitchen chair and sat next to Yunara. He glanced at his mum and bit his lower lip before starting. 'I was staying with my aunt and uncle for the weekend in Pembroke. Mum and Dad, and our little dog, Max, had gone to an exhibition.'

'It was an art exhibition; we were graphic artists,' Mrs Nailsworthy said, smiling. She nodded for Nails to continue.

He was silent for a few moments before taking a deep breath and going on. 'They were on their way back when there was a car crash ... Mum was badly injured but Dad and Max didn't survive.'

The twins stiffened, and Yunara gasped and put her hand on Nails' arm.

Sam's face remained blank. 'Was that why you were so nasty whenever Yunara or I mentioned our dads?'

Jenny felt her scalp tingle. 'Sam, you can't say things like that!'

Nails nodded. 'You're right, Sam. I was horrible to you.' He turned to Yunara. 'To the both of you ... I'm sorry.' He took a sip of his orange juice. 'I've been angry for a long time; angry that my dad and Max were taken away and angry that Mum lost her sight.'

Sam blinked rapidly. He was taking in every detail. 'Were you excluded from your other school because you were angry and nasty?'

Mrs Nailsworthy reached out and patted her son's arm. 'It was a very difficult time for Norman. I was in hospital for quite a while and then we had lots of people telling us that I wouldn't be able to look after him. It was so difficult, especially after losing his dad and little Max.'

Nails sat up straight. 'I didn't want lots of people with folders full of papers coming to our house to take us to meetings. Those places were always the same, horrible rooms with plain, white walls, smelling of disinfectant. There'd be a box of plastic toys in the corner, which they'd offer to me. I didn't want them, I wanted my own toys, and my own home and Max. I was angry and naughty, especially in school. But we managed at home, didn't we, Mum?'

'Yes, cariad, of course we did, and we're managing just fine now. We needed a fresh start so we moved here, to Barrowmarsh. I have someone call in a couple of times a week, just to make sure we have what we need, but we're more than capable of looking after ourselves. We didn't say too much to the school because we didn't want a fuss, and we didn't want to rely on others; we wanted to start out all over again.' Mrs Nailsworthy smiled.

Nails leaned forward, rested his chin on his hands and sighed. 'I was excluded from my last school and I suppose I deserved it. I was angry and nasty to everyone. I saw doctors and stuff, and they wanted to give me medicine to calm me down, but Mum wouldn't let them. We moved to Barrowmarsh to get away from all that. Things were better at home, but I was still horrible to everyone at school.'

Sam nodded. 'You called me Dumbo and Mummy's boy, and you were cruel to Yunara.'

Yunara thrust her hand out towards Nails and said quickly, 'Don't worry, I can understand exactly how bad you must have felt.'

'That's the thing,' Nails said, slowly nodding his head, 'you didn't know why I was so bad, yet you weren't nasty to me. You put up with me.' He shrugged his shoulders. 'Mr Frost has been brilliant, and Miss Bell has been to visit and has told me that when I'm old enough and she's retired she'll teach me to ride a motor bike. *And*,' he grinned, 'she'll even let me ride her Hog!'

Everyone laughed.

Jimmy watched as his sister took out her journal, scribbled a few lines then looked around the room. 'From now on we're all going to be the best of friends and treat each other really well.'

Mrs Nailsworthy put a finger to her chin. 'I'm sure you'll have your moments and your little quarrels but that's what happens with friends.'

Sam finished off his cake. 'Would you make another cake for us soon, please, Mrs Nailsworthy?'

'Yes, of course I will,' she laughed, and there was a little tear on her cheek. 'I'm sure Norman will help me.'

Nails grinned. 'I love baking cakes, and I'll do a double chocolate one with loads of chocolate buttons on top especially for you, Sam ... I should also make one for Mr Frost, and say sorry to him.'

'Mr Frost is nice. He lets me have badges, and his name is Freddy Frost, and he told Henry the Eighth, our hamster, that his name is Mr Frosty Wosty.'

Nails sat back in his chair and looked at the ceiling. 'I've been so horrible to him. I've been especially horrible whenever he's mentioned football, which, you have to admit, has been quite a lot.'

They all laughed again.

Nails held his mum's hand. 'The thing is ... my dad always took me to watch Newport County play. I absolutely loved going to the games, collecting programmes and getting the autographs of the players. Dad and I also watched lots of other teams on *Match of the Day*. My all-time favourite player is Leon Britton of The Swans ... but, without my dad, I haven't wanted to watch football. It reminds me how much I miss him, and it's so painful.'

Yunara passed Nails a drink of orange juice. 'We can all watch football together if you like.'

'Thank you, mate, I'd really like that.'

Yunara beamed. 'It'll help me, too!'

'And what about Max?' Jenny whispered. 'Is that why you rescued Teabag?'

Nails threw back his head and laughed. 'Yes, our Max was a little Scottie. He was my dog, and after losing him I was so jealous of you having a dog. Do you remember that day I picked on you by Druid's Pond? Teabag warned me off and chased me. When I fell over I was terrified he was going to bite me but, instead, he licked my face. It reminded me of Max; he was lovely, but a daft little thing, too!'

For the rest of the evening everyone chatted and enjoyed playing computer games. They talked about Teabag, school, chocolate cake, the octopus in the pond and The Thursdays' forthcoming cup match. Mrs Nailsworthy promised that she and Norman would be at the match, and would be shouting for the home team.

Jimmy went on about the qualities of Barrowmarsh players such as Jason Boyd, Bryn Williams, Geraint Morgan and Robbo Robinson. He detailed the strengths of Dylan Milkwood, Sahidol Ali and Joe Rogers. The twins talked about the unpredictable genius of Matthew Henderson and also mentioned how proud they were of their dad, Jack Jones. Everyone agreed, however, that the real star of the Barrowmarsh team was their veteran captain, Mr Freddy Frost.

Jenny told Mrs Nailsworthy all about her Treasure Book, and Yunara decided she'd start one too. Before the evening was over Nails demonstrated his skills and talent as a graphic artist on his Mum's Mac computer.

'I can't quite manage things myself, now,' Mrs Nailsworthy said, 'but I've taught Norman a few things and he's been a quick learner.'

Everyone looked at Nails' artwork and said how brilliant it was.

Jenny jotted something in her journal. 'I've made a note, Nails, that you should show everyone your pictures during Circle Time.'

He blushed, and tugged the collar of his T-shirt. 'Thank you, diolch ... oh, by the way, I've made a few things for you.' He brought out a large folder. 'I printed these this afternoon.'

They were delighted with their gifts. Nails had made posters of Barrowmarsh Thursdays Football Club for the twins, with pictures of all the players surrounding the club's emblem. There was a large poster of Spiderman for Jandir and another of British and African wild animals for Yunara. For Sam, Nails had designed and printed a set of badges illustrated with a selection of dinosaurs.

Everyone was thrilled, and by the time Sam's dad called to collect them they knew that things would be a lot different from then on.

Some things, however, would never change. Jenny scribbled furiously in her Treasure Book, recording every detail of the evening's events; Sam held out his hand to show his dad his new badges, and Jimmy's thoughts turned to the biggest match in the history of Barrowmarsh Thursdays Football Club.

Chapter Eleven

With the New Year came the excitement of the FA Cup third-round, and the frightening reality of The Thursdays playing against one of the world's most powerful and famous football clubs.

The day that everyone had been waiting for arrived at last. It was bitterly cold but every so often a beam of sunlight cut through the gloomy January sky and sparkled on the frosty grass outside the back door of Druid's Lodge.

Jimmy sat on the doorstep with a piece of peanut-butter covered toast between his teeth as he struggled to pull on his trainers. Teabag bounced around him, wagging his tail and yapping excitedly.

'Come on, slowcoach,' Jenny nagged, 'hurry up.'

'Stupid trainers,' Jimmy mumbled through his soggy toast.

'Well, it would help if you untied the laces first.'

He glared at his sister with half-closed eyes as he managed to push his right foot into the shoe. He chewed his toast ferociously and jammed his left foot into the other trainer.

Jenny attached Teabag's lead and they all walked down the path at the side of the guest house, crossed the road and strolled towards the village green.

'Morning, Mr Rogers,' Jenny called to the tall man loading a few bags of cement onto the back of his pick-up truck. 'I suppose you're ready for the big game today?'

Joe Rogers played as a striker for The Thursdays. Grandad called him a centre-forward, which is what they were called, Jimmy guessed, before teams had strikers, lone strikers, holding strikers, wide strikers, target men, and supporting attackers playing in the hole at the head of the diamond! He wasn't quite sure what it all meant but he'd heard Dad using those terms during his team-talks. He decided that football must have been easier back in his grandad's time!

Joe grinned at the twins. 'I wouldn't miss it for the world, kids. Just have a little patio and wall job to finish off first; then I'll be back by eleven o'clock, raring to go.'

Bella, Joe's wife, walked over to the truck and handed her husband a bag of sandwiches and a flask. 'Mind you don't hurt yourself this morning and miss the game.' She playfully knocked his woolly hat down over his eyes.

He grinned at her. 'So you're not joining me on this job then?' He turned to the twins and added, 'My Bella is the best brick-layer in Wales.'

'True,' she said, 'but I'm on swimming duty this morning, and you'd better make sure you're back as soon as possible.'

Suddenly, there was an explosion of noise – laughter, screeches, shouts and the clattering of shoes on the pavement, like ten skeletons kick-boxing in a biscuit tin, as Joe and Bella's four children ran down the path to greet them and to pat a tail-wagging Teabag. They were going swimming but were more excited about getting back in time to see their dad playing in the big cup match.

'We're off to set up the scoreboard,' Jimmy explained. 'See you later.'

The Rogers' children waved to the twins, to Teabag and to their dad as they climbed into *Violet*, their mum's vintage VW camper van.

On match days Jimmy and Jenny always went over to Parc y Derwydd to put the names of the teams onto the scoreboard and to get the box of numbers ready.

'Do you think we'll ever get an electronic scoreboard here?' Jenny asked.

Jimmy raised his eyebrows. 'Hey, this is Barrowmarsh, remember, not Barcelona!'

As they walked onto the village green, Geraint Morgan cycled past, whistling cheerfully; his post-bag full of mail slung across his shoulders.

'Morning, Geraint, good luck in today's game.'

He raised his hand in a casual wave, then carried on whistling as he cycled up towards the High Street. Geraint had been the team's goalkeeper for nearly twenty years.

The village green looked completely different. Preparations for the big match had started the week before, with trucks delivering all sorts of things to the football ground. During the previous afternoon, a fleet of 'SkySports' lorries and vans had trundled down the High Street and were now parked on The Green, next to the high, temporary fences that surrounded Parc y Derwydd.

Jenny explained who they were to the policeman guarding a new gateway marked 'Players and officials'. He had to speak to someone on his crackly radio before he would let them through. They walked into the ground and gawped at the unfamiliar rows of temporary seating.

They'd heard the clattering and clanging, shouting and banging all week, but couldn't have imagined such huge changes.

The twins ducked under the perimeter fence and took a short cut across the pitch while Teabag bounced around, as usual. They waved to Dan Williams, the Groundsman, who was pulling a heavy roller over the goalmouth away to their right. They also shouted 'Bore da!' to Mair, Dan's wife, who was busy unpacking boxes and getting everything ready in the club's small, pitch-side snack bar.

Jenny climbed the rickety wooden steps to the small space behind the scoreboard. Jimmy followed and started rummaging through the large box of team names. 'Barrowmarsh' was already in place on the scoreboard. He removed the name of Caradoc Warriors, their last league opponents, from the scoreboard and slotted the 'Visitors' name-board into place.

The morning skittered by and people seemed to appear from nowhere. The whole village, The Green and the shops bubbled into life. Thick cables snaked away from the television trucks and disappeared under the fences surrounding the football ground. One large, grey lorry had three enormous white satellite dishes on top which, Grandad had told them, would be used to transmit live pictures from their very own village to towns and cities all over the world.

This was FA Cup third-round day, and the excitement and tension was building like cling-film stretched over a crackling bowl of Rice Krispies. The village youngsters watched with excitement as police officers on tall, powerful horses patrolled the High Street.

Street vendors were busily setting up their stalls. Huge numbers of scarves, flags, balloons and souvenirs were being piled and tied onto stands. Burger vans and chip vans, pizza, vegetarian, speciality food, ice-cream and a whole lot of other vans jostled for parking spaces on the High Street and all around the village green.

By mid-day, crowds of people, far more than the number that lived in the village, had gathered along Barrowmarsh High Street waiting for the arrival of United's team bus and a chance to catch a glimpse of the world-famous footballers. Just after a quarter past twelve the thrum and buzz of the crowd swelled to a cheering roar, like thunder rumbling around the village. Within a minute the flashing blue lights of police cars and bikes appeared, moving slowly through the narrow, crowded street. The gleaming white and red coach slid majestically into view, and the people lining the route cheered and waved at the well-known players who were partly hidden behind the darkened glass of the bus.

Jimmy looked across at the metal barriers and the army of police officers that stood between Druid's Lodge and the hordes of visiting people. It dawned on him that their home was going to be a changing room for the famous United players! It would also, of course, be the base for The Thursdays' players. The only other people who were allowed to get anywhere near Druid's Lodge were Barrowmarsh residents. Villagers, the twins included, had to wear special badges so that police officers and security staff could identify them.

A barrier-gate was pulled back to allow the United team-coach and its police escorts to pass through and glide over to the Jones' home.

Jenny and Jimmy bobbed about excitedly at a bedroom window to see over the cordon of police officers that surrounded their house, and Teabag yapped wildly. They were under strict orders to keep him out of the way while the United players and staff were in Druid's Lodge. They peered through the window then held their breath as the bus door slid open. A young man wearing red headphones emerged from the coach.

'*That's … That's …*' Jenny squealed. '*Where's my mobile? I simply have to take a photo and send it to all my friends*!'

One by one they appeared: international footballers from Wales, England, Scotland, Northern Ireland, the Republic of Ireland and almost every other country imaginable. These were faces that the twins had seen so often on television, in magazines and in their collection of *Premier Star* cards … This was like a dream. Jenny was speechless. She rapidly tapped the keypad of her phone, and Teabag whirled around the bedroom, chasing his tail.

Jenny nudged her brother; they could hear Mum's voice as she led United's officials and players to the large dining room, usually reserved for residential guests. She'd organised a buffet lunch for the visitors to enjoy, after they had been formally greeted by Miss Bell, of course.

After lunch the United squad were taken to a couple of guest rooms so that they could change into their kits.

The players then gathered at the front door where stewards and police were waiting to escort them over to the football pitch for a warm-up.

The twins had lunch in the kitchen, making sure, of course, that Teabag was with them and not causing mischief elsewhere. He seemed happy enough and sat in his basket, chewing contentedly on an old slipper that Grandad had given him. As the time for the start of the match crept nearer they slipped out of the kitchen, closed the door tightly behind them and went to stand at the entrance of the lounge, where the Barrowmarsh players had gathered for the manager's team-talk ...

'You have to believe in yourselves.' The twins could hear Dad's growling voice. 'This is the biggest event in our long and proud history ... Just imagine it,' he was almost whispering now, 'we're in the FA Cup third-round ... The F ... A ... Cup, and the name of Barrowmarsh Thursdays is there, alongside West Ham, Cardiff City, Swansea City, Liverpool, Chelsea and today's opponents ...' He paused, swallowed and almost gasped, ' ... United!'

The room was silent. Jenny peeped around the door and noticed that everyone seemed to be gazing into space and viewing their own, private daydream.

Dad looked around the room, making eye-contact with every single upturned face. 'Today, gentlemen, we are making Barrowmarsh history ... let's go out there and make national, no, international history!'

Jenny and Jimmy held their breath as they stood in the doorway. They'd listened to many team-talks before; the football club had been a part of their lives for as long as they could remember. This team-talk, however, was different!

They jumped, like sparrows startled by the clatter of bin-lids on rubbish-collection day, as Dad's voice suddenly boomed out. 'BUT WE HAVE TO WIN AGAINST UNITED THIS AFTERNOON TO TAKE OUR PLACE IN THE HISTORY BOOKS ... WE HAVE TO BEAT THEM ... Otherwise...' he looked around the room with a pained expression on his face ... 'we will be forgotten for all eternity!' He paused, looked to the ceiling, took a deep breath and held his arms wide. 'ONCE MORE INTO THE BREACH, MY BRAVE WARRIORS ... WHEN WE STEP ONTO THE HALLOWED TURF THIS AFTERNOON, LET US GO OUT THERE TO WIN ... LET US GO OUT THERE TO WIN IN STYLE ...' He sat down. The room was silent, and after a moment's pause he added, quietly and slowly, 'Dear friends, this ... is ... *our* ... time.' The twins jumped as he leapt to his feet and thumped the table. 'LET'S GO OUT THERE AND MAKE BARROWMARSHERS WEEP WITH PRIDE!'

The room erupted in a fury of deafening and back-slapping cheers. Teabag, who'd been left in the kitchen, busily but quietly demolishing a slipper, started barking frantically at the sudden uproar from the lounge.

At last, the time arrived for everyone to take their places over at Parc y Derwydd. Seats in the temporary stand had been reserved for the regulars. The kitchen of Druid's Lodge was a flurry of black and white scarves, hats, rosettes and balloons as Jenny and Jimmy, their mum and grandparents prepared to leave.

'Now make sure Teabag is safely and securely tucked away out of harm's reach when we leave.' Mum issued the instruction as she pulled her gloves on and tucked her hair into her woolly hat.

'Yes, Mum.'

Teabag was in his basket, one paw on the half chewed slipper, guarding it jealously as he gnawed on a large, fresh bone, bought especially for the occasion.

Jenny patted Teabag's head. 'That should keep him occupied and out of mischief.'

They stepped outside; Jimmy stood and watched as Mum pulled the door, checked it was shut properly, and when she was satisfied that all was secure they set off across The Green.

As they approached the tall, temporary fence, with tickets in hand, Jenny suddenly screamed. 'My Treasure Book ... I've forgotten my Treasure Book!'

'It doesn't matter,' said Mum, 'we're going to a football match, you're not going to need it.'

'Oh, but I might,' Jenny flapped, 'you never know when a good word might suddenly appear.'

Jimmy nodded his agreement. 'You never know.'

Mum stopped, sighed, and rubbed the back of her neck. 'Don't be silly, Jennifer, you can do without it for an hour or so.'

'*But I can't,*' Jenny wailed, '*I most definitely can't do without it ... I never go anywhere without it.*'

'She doesn't,' Jimmy giggled.

Mum glanced at her watch and handed Jenny the house-keys. 'Well you'd better run back and get it, then. Use the back door, and hurry up, we need to get into the ground and into our seats before the teams come out.'

Jenny ran back across the village green. Within a few minutes she'd returned, panting and clutching her Treasure Book like a comfort blanket.

'Thank goodness for that,' said Mum, 'now, can we please get inside? Come on, quickly, Dad will expect us to be there, cheering, when The Thursdays run onto the pitch. By the way, Jennifer, did you make sure the back door was shut properly when you left the house?'

Jenny's eyes flickered from side to side. Then she looked down, avoiding Mum's questioning gaze. 'Yes ... um, yes, of course I did.'

'Did you?' Jimmy whispered.

'Yes, I did, definitely.' She frowned. 'I *think* I did.'

Chapter Twelve

Jimmy was wide-eyed as he looked around the packed Parc y Derwydd. 'Where's our little football ground gone?'

Jenny gasped. 'Wow! It didn't look or sound anything like this when we were here earlier.'

That morning they'd seen the barriers, temporary stands and television lorries. They'd seen technicians pulling and hoisting platforms and cables, and others setting up microphones. They'd even watched as engineers fixed mini railway tracks alongside the pitch for mobile television cameras.

This was different. Earlier, the ground had been almost empty, and fairly quiet, apart from the occasional sound of a drill, the clatter of hammers and spanners, and the echoing chatter of people working with the television crews. Now that the ground was crammed full of chanting and shouting spectators waving flags, banners and scarves it looked so much bigger, and the noise was something they were simply not used to.

They were delighted to see Nails sitting on the end of the front row, decked out in a black and white scarf and hat. They greeted Mrs Nailsworthy warmly and welcomed her to Parc y Derwydd. They were also delighted to see Yunara, and to learn that she had volunteered to be the match commentator for Nails' mum. They all promised to meet up later that evening.

The twins followed as their mum led everyone to the

centre of the front row of the grandstand where seats had been reserved for them. They realised that this would be the first time they'd ever sat down to watch Barrowmarsh play. It felt, Jimmy thought, just like walking along the rows in the cinema, except it wasn't dark.

'Excuse me,' Mum said, as people stood so that they could pass between the seats and the fence directly in front.

'So sorry, thank you very much,' Grandma apologised, as she moved slowly along the row, nodding to friends and neighbours.

'Hello, Wayne,' Grandad said to Mr Braine, The Sarcastic Clapper, 'glad to see you've decided to join us in the posh seats.'

Mr Braine folded his arms and looked grim. 'Might as well have a little bit of comfort, we won't get much joy once the match starts.'

'Now, now, Wayne, let's be a little more optimistic; it's just eleven men against eleven men. Anything could happen.'

Mr Braine shook his head and scowled. 'Lambs to the slaughter, you mark my words; lambs to the slaughter!'

Grandad winked at the twins.

'Epic,' Jenny shouted as they took their seats. She was looking at the glossy match-day programme. 'This is the Barrowmarsh team; these are all people we know, and look, here's Dad's name ... centre-back and player-manager.'

Jimmy scanned the programme and was thrilled to read Dad's name alongside Geraint Morgan, Morlais Jenkins, Jason Boyd and Bryn Williams. He was delighted to see Mr Frost listed in midfield with Matthew Henderson, and noted that Robbo Robinson, Sahidol Ali, Dylan Milkwood and Joe Rodgers would also start the match.

'Not a bad line-up!' he commented.

'Hmm, maybe,' Jenny agreed, 'but look at the names on the other side; we've got them all in our Premier Stars sticker collection. Every one of them is really, really, stupendously famous ...' She found it hard to believe that in a very short while they'd actually be watching the likes of Serge Petranovic, the Russian goalkeeper, together with Micky Flynn, Klaus Schwarz, Didier Pascal and Robbie Hamilton – megastars from Ireland, Germany, France and Scotland.

Jimmy studied United's line-up. 'The three central midfielders, Walsingham, Dudley and Cecil are all England regulars.'

'Yes,' said Jenny, 'and Bob Dudley is the Queen's favourite footballer!'

'What? Dudley is Queen Elizabeth's favourite?'

'He sure is, I'm certain I read it somewhere.'

Jimmy chewed on his finger, nervously. 'But what about their forward-line? Juliano, Brazil's right-winger, Ryan Gower of Wales out on the left flank, and their star Italian striker, Fabio Borano up front ... wow!'

'Lambs to the slaughter, you mark my words, lambs to the slaughter!' Mr Braine shook his head and repeated his grim warning.

Suddenly, a voice boomed out from the huge loud-speakers that had been set up along the front of the grandstand. 'Ladies and gentlemen, boys and girls, croeso i Parc y Derwydd ... welcome to this momentous and historic occasion, the FA Cup third-round.'

There were cheers, whistles and applause from the big crowd.

'The players and officials are lining up and are almost ready to take the field,' the announcer continued.

Everyone looked towards the tunnel at the centre of the grandstand. People with hand-held television cameras, microphones and cables buzzed and tumbled around the tunnel entrance...

'Would you please welcome ...' the voice echoed around the ground as the noise increased to a loud and excited rumble ... 'The legendary ... *U ...NI ...TED*!'

The rumble grew until it sounded like the roar of an on-rushing express train.

'And,' the announcer said, pausing for dramatic effect, 'please give a special welcome to your very own heroes ... *BARROWMARSH THURSDAAAAAAAYS*!'

Everyone leapt to their feet and the thunderous noise was like nothing ever before heard in the sleepy little village. Jimmy could see that Sam, who sat a few seats along, had his hands over his ears. The twins knew that he didn't like loud noises or crowds of people, and they saw that he was rocking back and forth in his seat. His mum was talking to him calmly and getting him to slowly count the fingers on her gloved hand. Mr Frost sometimes did that with Sam at school and explained that it was a way of getting him to think about something familiar and safe.

Jenny was bouncing up and down beside her brother and waving her scarf. '*Come on Thursdays*!'

The referee and assistants emerged from the tunnel, followed by the team captains, mascots and players. Next to the red-shirted United captain, Robert Dudley, walked their very own teacher and Barrowmarsh captain, Mr Frost.

Miss Bell's voice boomed out. 'GO ON FREDDY, GET STUCK IN; CLOSE 'EM DOWN AND DON'T GIVE 'EM AN INCH ...'

'Steady on, Nell,' Grandad chuckled, 'they haven't started yet.'

Everyone laughed, but Miss Bell took no notice and carried on bellowing out instructions to the white-shirted players. Mr Frost shook hands with the match officials then led his team along the United line, shaking hands with every one of the famous players.

'Lucky Dad,' Jenny called to Jimmy over the noise of the crowd, 'he's getting to meet all those stars ... I simply must text my friends to tell them what he's doing.'

'Don't be daft, are you twp or something? All your friends are here, they can see what he's doing.'

'So they are, silly me.'

Dad looked over to the stand and waved to everyone as the players ran to their half of the field for a last minute warm up. The family cheered wildly and waved back. Mum turned to the people in the row behind and pointed towards the pitch. 'That's my husband out there, you know.'

'We know that, Jayne,' a man replied, 'we've been living in the village for the last thirty years!'

Grandad chuckled again and winked at the twins.

Jimmy nudged Jenny and pointed; Mr Frost was

standing with Bob Dudley, the United captain, the referee and his assistants in the centre circle. A coin had been tossed and the referee indicated that Barrowmarsh should kick-off. The United players took their positions and Mr Frost called the Barrowmarsh players together and gathered them in a huddle for his final captain's pep-talk. Everyone in the crowd stood, roared out their encouragement and clapped furiously until the players dispersed and ran to their starting places ...

Now this is where the story started, back on the first page, when the twins were feeling nervous in a tummy-churning, sickly sort of way, because they believed their team was going to get slaughtered.

Out on the pitch the officials checked their watches once more; the players stood ready for the start, and everyone waited for that shrill blast of the whistle that would mean the biggest match in the history of Barrowmarsh Thursdays Football Club was finally under way.

Mr Braine stood, took off his hat and spoke in a loud and serious voice. 'To those who are about to die, we salute you!' Everyone sitting nearby roared with laughter but Mr Braine just shook his head glumly.

Matthew Henderson and Joe Rogers stood over the ball; Mr Frost clapped his hands and shouted encouragement to his team mates. The referee looked to both assistants, glanced at his watch and put the whistle to his lips. The sound was lost in a deafening roar as Matthew tapped the ball to Joe, and Barrowmarsh got the match under way.

For a full five minutes the Thursdays kept possession, passing the ball sweetly, knocking it back to Geraint Morgan in the Barrowmarsh goalmouth who, in turn, was content to roll it out to the defenders. Mr Frost was doing a fine captain's job, and the twins could easily read his signs and gestures. He was telling his players to relax, slow things down and keep hold of the ball. United seemed happy to stroll around and wait for an opportunity to gain possession. Suddenly, Gower, their winger, intercepted a pass, played a beautiful ball through to Fabio Borano and then ran into space for the return pass, only twenty metres from goal. The winger unleashed a vicious shot with the outside of his boot. Jimmy held his breath; Jenny gripped her brother's arm and the crowd gasped as Geraint somehow managed to get a finger to the ball to tip it over the crossbar ... A corner to United!

The next fifteen minutes seemed to be a blur of action with United launching endless crosses and passes into the Barrowmarsh goalmouth. The frantic home team's players – all eleven of them – were heading, kicking and scrambling the ball absolutely anywhere so long as it was away from danger ... outside the posts, over the bar, high into the air and even into the crowd.

'Our players look exhausted,' said Grandad, 'and they've only played a quarter of the match!'

'Lambs to the slaughter,' Mr Braine muttered, 'lambs to the slaughter.'

Miss Bell got up from her seat, threw down her match-day programme and strutted to the front of the grandstand. 'GET A GRIP, BARROWMARSH. DON'T

LET THESE OVER-PAID NAMBY-PAMBIES GET THE BETTER OF YOU ... SHOW 'EM WHO'S BOSS!'

'United are so lucky that Miss Bell isn't out there playing for the team,' Jenny said, and Grandad grinned and winked at her.

'YOUNG HENDERSON,' Miss Bell screeched, 'DON'T STAND THERE LIKE A LEMON ... GO LOOKING FOR THE BALL; TAKE SOME PRESSURE OFF OUR DEFENCE!'

At that moment, Juliano, United's Brazilian right winger, took a pass near to the touchline. As he controlled the ball he looked up at Miss Bell, raised an eyebrow, and smirked.

'AND YOU CAN STOP THAT RIGHT NOW, YOUNG MAN. DON'T YOU *DARE* LOOK AT ME IN THAT TONE OF VOICE!'

Juliano shook his head and stared, and the distraction was enough for Matthew Henderson to nip in, take the ball from the Brazilian's feet and set off on a dazzling run down the left wing. The crowd stood and roared, as Henderson's superb cross was headed just over the United bar by Dylan Milkwood.

'NOT A BAD EFFORT, BUT IT SHOULD HAVE GONE UNDER, MILKWOOD. STILL, NEVER MIND, THAT'S THE SPIRIT, GET STUCK IN, BARROWMARSH; SHOW 'EM WHAT WE'RE MADE OF.' Miss Bell boomed.

The crowd erupted into life and started to chant, 'COME ON THURSDAYS, COME ON THURSDAYS ...'

The attack on the United goalmouth, together with the crowd's chanting, seemed to instantly lift the team and give them confidence. Dad was winning everything in the air against Borano, Italy's number one striker; Mr Frost was like a terrier in midfield, unsettling Cecil and Dudley, winning tackles and spraying passes in all directions, and Sahidol was showing some lovely skills out on the right-wing. Jenny pointed out that he was consistently getting the better of Hamilton, United's full back. United were being forced to play deeper in their own half and to defend more than they would have expected.

The first half seemed to fly by and when the referee blew the whistle for half-time, the Barrowmarsh faithful were overjoyed that there was no score; they could hardly believe it, they were still holding the mighty United to a draw. The players left the field for a well-earned break and to a standing ovation from the ecstatic and excited crowd.

The twins met Nails, Sam, Yunara and Jandir at half time. Everybody was talking about how well the team was doing to be on level terms at the half-way stage of the game. Even Mr Braine seemed to have a funny little smile on his face but the twins noted that he was still muttering, 'Lambs to the slaughter,' and 'Don't count your chickens!'

Jenny and Jimmy left their friends and moved down to the rail surrounding the pitch, where Mr Hamlet Horton was huffing and puffing and wiping his red face with a handkerchief. He had moved Miss Bell's Throne to the side of the pitch, next to the trainer's and substitutes' bench. Jimmy grinned and nudged his sister when he saw that the caretaker was doing his soliloquy and grumbling about how a man couldn't even have a bit of peace and quiet on his day off.

The tannoy announcer's voice suddenly cut into the music that was playing, and echoed out. '*Ladies and gentlemen, boys and girls, the teams are about to re-enter the field for the second half ...*' Once again the foot-stomping, hand-clapping, rumbling roar of the crowd boomed and rolled across Parc y Derwydd, and the twins were thrilled to see the famous red-shirted players jog out alongside their own team, only a few feet from where they were standing!

'*Dad!*' they shouted, and he put his thumb up and grinned at them.

'He looks confident, bro.'

Jimmy smiled. 'So he should, we're holding the world's most famous team to a draw, and half the match has gone already!'

Jenny nodded her agreement as they watched the players take up their positions. They were close enough to the pitch to hear Dad and Mr Frost calling out instructions and encouragement.

'*Freddy,*' the twins heard Dad shout to Mr Frost, 'don't forget, your job in midfield is to break down their movement; don't let them play their passing game through the middle ... Keep an eye on Walsingham.'

'Right you are, boss,' Mr Frost responded.

'Sahidol, Robbo,' Dad continued, 'drop back when you have to, and stay tight to their wingers ... get the tackles in quickly and let them know you're there!'

Sahidol raised his hand. 'Got you, gaffer.'

Robbo Robinson nodded. 'Okay boss.'

'REMEMBER LADS,' Miss Bell thundered, 'IT'S ELEVEN AGAINST ELEVEN; IT'S OUR PITCH AND WE'VE GOT THEM REALLY WORRIED!'

The headmistress was standing next to her Throne, near the touchline. Hamlet Horton was standing behind her, mumbling his soliloquy, but the twins couldn't hear what he was saying.

'Miss Bell is using psychology,' Jenny told her brother, 'she's trying to make our players think they're better than United.'

'But it's not true, sis, so is she telling a fib or being sarcastic?'

'It's neither, it's ... it's ... psychology ... positive thinking!'

'That is *so* not fair,' Jimmy complained. 'It's another thing for us to remember ... and there's no way I'll be able to remember how to spell psychology.'

Jenny laughed as she and her brother turned their attention to the pitch where Borano and Dudley stood over the ball, ready to re-start the match. The referee counted the players on each side, checked his watch, waved to his assistants and blew the whistle to get the second half under way.

Chapter Thirteen

United started the second half with determination; a few slick passes and an attack was launched down their left flank. The red shirted Juliano shuffled his feet, flicked the ball to his right and sped past Robbo Robinson with ease. The crowd gasped, but Mr Frost slid into a tackle and managed to push the ball off the winger's foot and out of play for a corner to United.

'Uh-oh,' Jimmy said, 'Dad looks annoyed.'

Out on the pitch Dad yelled as he ran back into a defensive position. 'Sahidol, Robbo, What did I just say? Stay close to their wingers; keep goal-side and stop them from running at us!'

'But he's Brazil's number one winger, boss ... and one of the top scorers in the Premier League.'

'Yes, and you're the best left-sided midfielder in Wales ... just remember that!'

Jenny nudged her twin. 'See, that's psychology, too!'

Jimmy didn't think that Robbo was convinced by Dad's positive thinking as he looked very, very nervous.

The corner was taken and Matthew Henderson managed to squeeze through a crowd of United players to head the ball out to the far touchline and to safety.

Another United cross was launched into the Barrowmarsh penalty area, this time Joe Rogers dropped back to help his defence by heading clear.

From the side of the pitch, the twins could hear Dad's instructions to his players. 'Geraint,' he called to the

Thursdays' goalkeeper, 'get out to their crosses; catch the ball, punch it clear, do whatever you have to, but you must command your penalty area ... Don't give them space or time to head the ball... you really must sort out those crosses.'

Geraint had gone very pale. Jenny gave Jimmy a knowing look and he nodded. Geraint was a good shot-stopper, but was often called 'Dracula' by his team-mates because he really didn't like crosses!

For ten minutes the match was a blur of relentless United attacks and pressure. Walsingham, Dudley and Cecil were showing their professional experience by controlling the midfield for the Premier League Champions, and the Barrowmarsh tackles were becoming more and more desperate. Shots from United were whistling past the post and skimming the crossbar. Geraint stopped a stinging effort from Borano with a spectacular dive to his left, tipping the ball around the post for another corner. Jason Boyd, the Thursdays' left back, managed to throw his body into the path of a thundering header from United's Klaus Schwarz to block an almost certain goal. Barrowmarsh now had eleven men defending inside their own penalty area, marking and tackling wave after wave of United attacks. At the other end of the field, Petranovic, United's Goalkeeper was little more than a spectator.

Miss Bell leapt out of her throne, and ignoring the protests from the fourth official, marched to the touchline. 'FOR GOODNESS SAKE, BARROWMARSH, GET A GRIP, SHOW SOME BOTTLE. TAKE THE GAME TO THEM; PRESS THEM FURTHER UP THE

PITCH. DON'T LET THEM PASS THE BALL AROUND!'

Sir Alec, United's famous manager, stood, and was about to complain, but sat down again as Miss Bell, hands on hips, turned and glared at him in that '*and you can stop that right now, my boy*' way that she was well-known for! Hamlet Horton whispered something to the headmistress. Her face turned red and she glared at the caretaker. 'YES, YES, MR HORTON, I KNOW WHO HE IS ... AND I CAN ASSURE YOU, HE WOULDN'T GET AWAY WITH CONTINUOUSLY CHEWING GUM IF HE WERE IN *MY* SCHOOL!'

Sir Alec slid down in his seat and tried to avoid Miss Bell's glare. Jenny and Jimmy looked at each other and sniggered before turning back to watch the action on the pitch. United were now totally dominant and the twins could see that their own players looked absolutely exhausted. Didier Pascal collected the ball in the centre-circle, played a pass to Cecil, took a return pass and, cleverly avoiding Sahidol's challenge, sent the red-shirted Ryan Gower on a run down the left wing. The tricky Welsh International outpaced Matthew Henderson and Mr Frost, dribbled around Jason Boyd and darted into the Barrowmarsh penalty area.

'This is it!' Jimmy gasped, 'He's going to score!'

Gower pulled back his foot for the shot, and they expected to see the net bulge but suddenly the home team's full-back Morlais Jenkins appeared from nowhere and slid into a tackle, sending the ball spinning out for a corner and temporary safety. The crowd roared and wildly applauded the sublime interception.

Miss Bell leapt into the air. 'THAT'S THE SPIRIT, YOUNG JENKINS; GET INTO 'EM!'

The corner kick was hoisted into the Barrowmarsh goal mouth; Dad managed to get his head to the ball and nod it over the bar for yet another United corner. This time, big Bryn Williams out-jumped Borano to head clear of the penalty area, but only as far as the Brazilian, Juliano, who controlled the ball skilfully on his chest, let it drop, then smashed a powerful volley toward goal. There was a moment of silence as everything seemed to move in slow motion ... Geraint Morgan dived, despairingly, as the ball swerved in mid-air and sailed over his out-stretched arms and finger-tips ...

A thud and a ping resonated around Parc y Derwydd and a split second later the crowd erupted into cheers and screams of delight. The crossbar shook from the impact of the ball, which then ricocheted into the crowd and to safety. Barrowmarsh were still in the game and still level with United!

The Premiership team continued to pass and probe for an opening; Barrowmarsh continued to tackle, press the United players and defend heroically. Miss Bell yelled and screamed with every kick!

Jenny nudged her brother and pointed to her watch. There were less than seven minutes left ... could they do it? Could they do the impossible and actually hold out for a draw with the World's greatest team?

Miss Bell knew that time was slipping away and was frantically calling instructions across the pitch. 'FREDDY, JACK, SLOW THINGS DOWN... JUST KEEP POSSESSION, RUN THE CLOCK DOWN ... THERE

ARE ONLY FIVE MINUTES LEFT ... DON'T DO ANYTHING DAFT!'

Now why is it, Jenny thought, that whenever someone says 'don't do anything daft', someone goes and does something daft?

United's Fabio Borano had received the ball just inside the Barrowmarsh penalty area; with three defenders around him he had no-where to go. He started to move away from goal in the hope of finding a team-mate to pass to.

'THAT'S IT, LADS,' Miss Bell encouraged, 'LET HIM GO; HE'S GOING AWAY FROM GOAL.'

Suddenly, disaster! Morlais Jenkins attempted to drag the ball from Borano but somehow managed to catch the Italian's ankle. The forward stumbled then crashed to the floor. The gasp from the crowd turned to a groan of disbelief as the referee gave a sharp blast of the whistle and pointed emphatically to the penalty spot!

Sir Alec leapt from the bench and punched the air in delight, and Miss Bell stood as if frozen to the spot. Her mouth was open but for once she was silent.

Jenny covered her face with her hands. 'This is so cruel, we were only a few minutes away from history ... just three or four minutes away from the most amazing draw, ever!'

For the first time in the game the noise of the crowd dropped to a quiet murmur. Jimmy looked over his shoulder and saw Mum holding a handkerchief to her red eyes and Grandad patting her shoulder. Even Mr Braine was stunned into a white-faced silence.

Jimmy looked back to the pitch and poked Jenny's

arm. 'Look, Frankie Walsingham has placed the ball on the penalty spot; he's going to take the kick for United.'

'Well, that's it then,' she muttered, miserably, 'he's the top spot-kick man in the Premier League.'

'Hey, what's Geraint doing?' Jimmy asked.

Out on the pitch, Geraint Morgan, the Barrowmarsh Goalkeeper, had walked from his goal-line and was standing right in front of Walsingham, who was waiting to take the kick. He started talking to the United player but the referee ordered him to move away and to take his place between the posts. Geraint turned away, then quickly turned back again, said something to the United player and laughed. The red-faced referee stomped over to the goalie and waved a yellow card.

Jenny nodded her head, and folded her arms. 'That's psychology *and* gamesmanship!'

'Is it?' Jimmy squinted and rubbed his chin. 'But Geraint's been booked by the ref.'

'Yes, but he's been trying to break Frankie Walsingham's concentration; he was doing his best to make him nervous and lose confidence.'

'How come you know so much, clever clogs?'

'Shush.' Jenny pointed to the pitch. 'Look, here we go, everyone's ready ...'

The United and Barrowmarsh players jostled each other on the edge of the penalty area. Geraint stood on his goal-line, flapping his arms up and down, and the referee gave the signal for the kick to be taken. Everyone in the crowd stood or sat motionless and some covered their eyes as Frankie Walsingham started his run-up. The United mid-fielder connected with his right foot and the thwack on the ball echoed around an almost silent Parc y Derwydd. The spinning ball sailed past Geraint's flailing fingers, heading for the bottom corner ... then there was a second thwack as the ball crashed against the inside of the post ... and rebounded into the arms of the startled but ever so grateful keeper. The little football ground exploded in an almighty cacophony of noise ... Barrowmarsh Thursdays were still in the game; United had missed the penalty!

Jimmy glanced behind and saw that Grandad was doing a little dance and had both thumbs in the air. Mum and Grandma were hugging. Mr Braine had his hands together, was looking up into the sky and was mouthing the words, 'Thank you, thank you,' over and over again.

Just then, the fourth official held up a digital board and the tannoy announcer confirmed that four additional minutes were to be played.

Sir Alec was on the edge of the technical area, frantically calling out instructions to his players, waving his arms and urging them to push forward for a winner.

Not to be outdone, Miss Bell strutted forward and bellowed, 'KEEP POSSESSION, BARROWMARSH; KEEP THE PASSES SHORT, SHUT THEM OUT. JUST A FEW MORE MINUTES AND WE'RE THERE.'

The next minute seemed like forever, with United throwing every player except their goalkeeper forward. Despite their obvious exhaustion, all eleven Barrowmarsh players were getting behind the ball, chasing, challenging and tackling. The crowd was clapping and chanting, '*THURSDAYS, THURSDAYS, THURSDAYS* ...'

Miss Bell was standing on the touchline, her black and white scarf held high above her head, cheering every tackle and shouting encouragement to each Barrowmarsh player in turn ...

'KEEP IT GOING, FREDDY ... THAT'S THE WAY, YOUNG HENDERSON ... WE'RE NEARLY THERE, JACK ... YOU'RE PLAYING A BLINDER, SAHIDOL ... GIVE 'EM SOME STICK, DYLAN MILKWOOD ...'

Everyone was on their feet; the United fans at the far end of the ground were roaring their team on. The Barrowmarsh supporters, filling three quarters of Parc y Derwydd, were willing their heroes to stay strong and to give just one last effort for the final minute or so.

'How long left?' Jimmy's legs wobbled and his tummy churned like there were a hundred spiders playing football inside him.

Jenny struggled to pull back her sleeve, her fingers shaking uncontrollably. Finally, she succeeded and was able to glance at her watch. 'Just one more m ... m ... minute. Do you think we'll do it? Do you think our little team will actually get a draw with the European Champions?'

Jimmy's mouth was too dry to answer.

Out on the pitch the ball ran loose near the halfway line. As the red-shirted Pascal ran towards it, Joe Rogers lunged into a clumsy tackle and the referee blew for a free kick to United. Sir Alec yelled to the goalkeeper, Petranovic, to come up to the half-way line to take the kick. The other ten red-shirted players rushed forward into the Barrowmarsh goal-mouth for what looked like being the last chance of the match.

Dad had his arms out-stretched, controlling and positioning his defensive line. Mr Frost was frantically barking out instructions to every one of his team-mates. Every United man was marked by a white shirted Thursdays player.

With the seconds trickling away, the big Russian Goalkeeper ran from his goal area and up to the halfway line. Without hesitating he hoofed the ball towards the Barrowmarsh goal. A crowd of players jumped but Geraint Morgan rose above them all, and with an almighty goal-keeper's punch sent the ball hurtling back towards the halfway line. The home crowd yelled in delight as the ball dropped into an open space.

'*OUT, OUT, OUT!*' Miss Bell was pulling on her hair and screaming.

The United players seemed to have frozen in disbelief at their failure to score and, in an instant, Dylan Milkwood raced onto the ball and looked up. He could see a completely open and un-guarded United goal fifty metres away. Petranovic, the United keeper, turned and frantically started to race back towards his goal area. Dylan took aim and walloped the ball with all the strength that remained in his weary legs.

There was an audible intake of breath from the crowd, followed by a white knuckled silence as the ball flew high into the air, sailed over the retreating goalkeeper, then dropped from the sky, spinning wickedly and heading directly towards the open United goal. Petranovic rushed after it, getting closer with every stride ...

The ball bounced and rolled into the penalty area

towards the gaping goal. The chasing Petranovic closed in to just three or four paces behind it, and was getting closer with every stride. Suddenly, there was an amber flash and a babble of excited yapping ...

'*TEABAG*!' Jenny and Jimmy yelled in horrified astonishment as their little dog leapt and bounced across the pitch in an excited, tongue-lolling, tail-wagging gallop.

Petranovic looked surprised and shocked. His head jerked around, his eyes boggled, and his mouth fell open as the noisy, woolly ball of mischief darted across his path. The Russian goalkeeper lost his balance, stumbled and sprawled head-first onto the grass ... The ball, even though it had lost its pace and had slowed down, trickled gently over the goal line ...

Silence gave way to the loudest uproar you could ever imagine. It was like ten thousand screaming kids playing British Bulldog in a bathroom! The ball nestled in the back of the net; the referee had blown his whistle and had pointed to the centre spot ... The goal had been given!

Dylan Milkwood was buried under a heap of Barrowmarsh players, while a delighted, barking Teabag darted and scurried around the pile.

Sir Alec complained angrily to the fourth official, who explained that the dog hadn't actually touched the goalkeeper or the ball, so no rule had been broken. Therefore, he confirmed, the goal was valid! The United players protested furiously but the referee stood firm, folded his arms, and waved them away.

After a few moments, Borano and Dudley re-started

the game, but almost immediately the referee looked at his watch, put the whistle to his lips and gave the signal that brought the match to an end. Barrowmarsh Thursdays had done the impossible ... they had beaten the World's most famous and most powerful team! They had beaten the Premier League and European champions! The team from the Welsh Central and Borders League, Division Three had knocked the mighty United out of the FA Cup!

The crowd was singing and dancing. The twins could see Mum, Grandad, Grandma and even Mr Braine laughing, singing and waving their scarves.

Miss Bell walked across to a shell-shocked Sir Alec. 'Bad luck, young man.' She shook his hand firmly. 'And if you're thinking of buying any of our players I can assure you that it'll cost you!'

Sir Alec, still chewing his gum, looked at the small, elderly headmistress. He blinked, scratched his cheek, chuckled and shook his head. 'I really don't know what to say ... Well done and good luck in the next round.'

Out on the pitch the players from both teams had swapped shirts; the United stars sportingly shook hands with the Barrowmarsh lads. The television crews, with their cameras, lights and microphones, were busy getting interviews from the victorious players. Several cameras and reporters had gathered around Dad, who was holding a smiley-faced Teabag in his arms. The cameras flashed as the little dog wagged his tail and adoringly licked his owner's face.

That night, lots of parties were held throughout the village, and the biggest of all was at Druid's Lodge.

Yunara, Jandir, Sam, Nails and his mum joined the twins, their family and the players of both teams. The youngsters managed to get the autographs of all the United players. Sir Alec gave Sam an official United club badge, and Didier Pascal talked to Jandir and Yunara about how he had grown up in Africa before being forced to leave his home and move to France.

The friends were delighted to be able to fill their autograph books. Not only did they get the United names, but they also got the signatures of the now famous Barrowmarsh players.

Nails insisted on having a paw-print from Teabag, and he spent most of the evening carrying the tail-wagging dog around with him and calling him a footballing legend.

And so ended the most memorable and astonishing day in the entire history of the little village of Barrowmarsh. As the twins chatted with Grandad, he told them he was certain that none of the villagers would ever forget the experience. Jenny wrote in her Treasure Book that the game would surely be remembered as the most remarkable match in the history of football.

Epilogue

After the United game, stories and pictures of the Thursdays, the players and their quaint village were splashed all over the national newspapers and magazines. Barrowmarsh also featured on several television programmes, with camera crews and interviewers popping up in every part of the village. They went to Druid's Lodge, where Mum and Dad and the twins were interviewed, and Miss Bell was only too pleased to show them around the school. She showed them where the famous Freddy Frost taught, and where stars such as Dylan Milkwood, Sahidol Ali and Matthew Henderson had sat during their school days.

The lively headmistress was photographed on her Hog, and Mr Hamlet Horton muttered and complained about all the vehicles in the school yard!

For a week or so, Teabag was a celebrity, with his picture smiling out from front pages up and down the country, along with headlines such as '*Teabag the Magnificent,*' and '*The FA Pup!*'

The twins were amazed at the number of letters and e-mails that arrived from all over the country. They included messages from lots of other football clubs. Jenny and Jimmy waded through congratulations from Swansea City, Cardiff City, Newport County, Wrexham and lots of other Welsh clubs. They even received supportive messages from many English teams.

The twins took the messages into school and Mr Frost suggested using them for a research project. He asked everyone to locate places on a map and to find out everything they could about those towns and cities, and about their sports teams in particular.

Mr Frost said that the Thursdays had exceeded all expectations. Jenny wrote that phrase in her Treasure Book and used it whenever she could ... when talking about her homework and her swimming ... And about Nails' swimming too!

After the United match, Barrowmarsh returned to normal – for a while! Mr Frost taught at the school, Geraint Morgan delivered the letters and parcels to the villagers, Sahidol Ali went to college, and Matthew Henderson continued to wear his baseball cap back-to-front! Nails was now very friendly with everyone and often went over to Druid's Lodge to watch television or to play games with Sam, Yunara and Jandir and the twins. He and his mum became fanatical supporters of the Thursdays ... but the thing he liked doing most of all was to take Teabag out for a walk.

Jenny continued to use her Treasure Book, of course, and one day, after chatting with Yunara, she put her reading book, *Pride and Prejudice* by Jane Austen, to one side, pulled out her trusty journal, chewed her pencil and scribbled ...

It is a truth, universally acknowledged, that Barrowmarsh is a small and quiet village. Days and months will come and go like smiles and frowns. We don't know what the future might hold but we will always have our wonderful memories ... our treasures!

And so, life went on. The youngsters of Ysgol Gynradd Cors-y-domen would often hear Miss Bell walking around the school, chuckling and singing to herself ... *'One Teabag Jones, there's only one Teabag Jones; one Teabag Jo-ones, there's only one Teabag Jo-ones ...'* And, she'd stopped calling the twins' little dog a *creature*, but referred to him from that time onward as a *luverlly, wuverlly, ickle pooch*!

As for the rest of the football season, perhaps you are thinking that Barrowmarsh Thursdays went on to win the FA Cup at Wembley ...

Well, that's another story!